WALK TO LOVE

Walk to Love

By
Larry W. Fish

E-Book Time, LLC
Montgomery, Alabama

Walk to Love

ISBN: 978-1-60862-577-2

First Edition
Published December 2014
E-BookTime, LLC
6598 Pumpkin Road
Montgomery, AL 36108
www.e-booktime.com

Chapter One

It was raining heavily in coastal South Carolina when Shane Donaldson ran from his car to the front door of his apartment. One of those thunderstorms had popped up out of the heat from the afternoon sun. Shane glanced back at his car thinking to himself that he was glad that he was able to park close to the front door. Shane had been living by himself since his wife of four years was killed in a car accident. They had just been getting on their feet financially and were talking of starting a family. The accident was devastating to Shane. It had turned a rugged, six foot four inch, two hundred and forty pound man from a happy man full of smiles. He was now a person that seldom spoke and cried himself to sleep every night.

The evening was just like any other. He made himself a sandwich and grabbed a beer. Shane had been having the same thing for supper for three years and two months. Becky always had a nice dinner on the table for him every night. She got off work about three hours before him and greeted him at the front door every day. As Shane was making his way to the sofa, he stopped and looked at the wedding photo. The tears started to flow just like they had so many times in the last few years. He whispered, "I love you, Becky. I love you so much."

He made his way to the sofa, sat down and ate his sandwich and drank his beer. He turned on the 6 o'clock news and saw where a young woman had been killed that day in a car accident. It made him think even more of Becky. He was wondering to himself if the young woman had been married. If she was, her husband's life would be changed forever. Friends had tried to get Shane to move on with his life, but every time they failed. They eventually stopped asking and he now had no one in his life.

Shane watched some TV and then went to bed early. It was a couple of hours before the tears stopped and Shane was finally able to doze off. Several hours later, Shane saw a huge flash of light and he sat right up in bed. Had it been lightening? Was it a dream? Shane wasn't sure but it was strange. As he was now sitting up in bed, he saw a vision in front of him. It was of him walking. He had a backpack on. Soon, he was back to sleep. The rest of the night went peaceful for Shane, but when he woke up, he just stayed in bed for the longest time thinking of the vision he had seen.

It seemed so real, like something was pushing him. Something was trying to tell him that he had to make a change in his life. He had never been a religious man but from his bed he said, "What is it God? What do you want me to do?"

He felt a hand rest on his shoulder as a voice said to him, "I will tell you when it is time. You will be going on a journey." Shane felt fear and peacefulness come over him at the same time.

The next several days were just like any other ordinary day. He couldn't help but think that it was all a mistake or a dream. He just went on every day like he had for the last few years. The only time he could smile was when he looked at their wedding photo. It was the happiest day of their young lives.

Chapter Two

It was a week or so later on a Saturday morning that Shane woke up and went into the bathroom. He ran his hand over his face and realized it was time for him to shave. He ran hot water into the sink and lathered his face. He remembered that Becky always liked it when he finished shaving. "You feel so smooth. I love a clean shaven face," she would say. It brought a faint smile to his face as he started to shave. Removing the stubble from his face, he washed off his face before applying some after shave. He moved his hands over his face and realized that Becky was always right; it did feel better.

As Shane ran some more hot water into the sink, the mirror fogged up from the steam. He took a little towel and started to clean the mirror off. As soon as he rubbed a little spot on the mirror, he saw Becky's face staring back at him. He jumped back startled and took another look in the mirror. Becky was smiling at him. She said, "I miss you, Shane. I love you so much. I'm at peace now and I want you to move on in your life."

Tears were running down Shane's face. He said, "I'll never love anyone but you, Becky."

Becky shook her head and said, "No Shane, it is time for you to move on. You need to be happy. You need to love again."

Shane felt that if he ever loved another woman it would mean that he didn't love Becky anymore. Becky told him that their love would always be in their hearts. She made him promise her that it was time for him to move on. Shane moved his lips close to the mirror and they gave a final kiss. As he moved away, he saw tears running down Becky's face. Becky's face faded away in the mirror. Shane just stared at it for a few minutes wondering if he was going crazy. He didn't think it was possible that he could actually see Becky's spirit in the mirror but he knew he had.

Shane spent the rest of that day thinking about Becky and what she had said to him. Deep down in his heart, he knew that she was right. He had a lot of life to live yet and he knew that Becky wanted him to be happy. He needed to hold someone close, give her a soft passionate kiss, and make love to her like he had with Becky so many times. He knew that the shame of loving another was something he couldn't think of any longer. He stood looking at their wedding photo and said, "Thank you, Becky. I love you." He wondered how many times he had said those words to her. She had showed more love to him than anyone deserved. The memories of their life together would always be in his heart.

Life went on for Shane. He had a couple of dates with some nice women but he just didn't feel the love. There was no spark – no shooting stars – and Shane knew that someday he would find that next someone in his life. God had told him quite a long time ago that he would be going on a journey. Shane was sitting at the table having a cup of coffee, wondering what He had meant by that. Did it mean he would be going on a journey of finding someone to love or did it mean he would be physically traveling somewhere? Shane thought of that every day. We all know that God has a plan for us and it kept Shane trying to figure out what that plan would be. He had no idea when or what would happen, but he knew that something was in the works for him.

Chapter Three

It was less than a month later when Shane was woken from a sound sleep. He was being pushed on his shoulder and he heard the words: "Wake up, Shane." Shane sat up in bed, rubbed his eyes and saw God standing next to him. Shane was startled and he just stared at the vision. He seemed unable to speak but it didn't matter because God would be doing most of the talking. God said, "We need to talk and we need to do it now." Shane asked what it was that they needed to talk about.

"Remember, Shane, that I told you some time ago that you would be going on a journey?" God said. Shane nodded his head. Shane was told that it was now time to prepare for that trip. God said, "You will be walking, Shane. It will be a great distance for you and it will take months." Shane inquired as to why he had to walk. Why couldn't he drive to where he needed to go? God smiled and said, "Because you need a lot of time to think. You have to start thinking about what is ahead of you and not what you have left behind. Oh sure, you will never forget Becky and you never should."

"Get yourself a backpack, a lightweight tent, a good pair of hiking shoes, some food to carry along and take some money with you," God said. He told Shane that he didn't know exactly when he would be starting on his journey but it would be soon. "I'll let you know when it is time and the direction you will be going. Now, go back to sleep and get yourself some rest," God told him.

Shane lay back down on the bed. It was deep into the night but his eyes were wide open and would stay that way until the sun started to come up over the horizon. For hours, he was thinking that maybe he was just hallucinating. How could this be happening to him? He had questions, so many questions that he needed to know before he started his walk. Was God going to tell him where he was going? Would he be in danger? Was this journey going to change his life forever? How long would the hike take him? Question after question just kept popping into his mind.

It didn't seem possible that he was talking to God. God was actually in his bedroom sitting on the edge of the bed telling him of a journey. He got up around seven in the morning and made his way to the bathroom. He washed up and shaved, wondering if a vision would show up in the mirror. He was really hoping that Becky would show her face again. He wanted to see her face one more time so badly but he was disappointed when it didn't happen. He stared into the mirror for the longest time hoping for a miracle.

Shane made his way to the kitchen. He put on some coffee. He really needed a cup after the night he had. He enjoyed the coffee along with a bowl of cereal topped off with some fresh blueberries. Having some breakfast did make him feel a lot better. Still, he sat at the kitchen table for the longest time just staring off into the distance.

Would he be returning home after the journey or would he have to clean out the apartment and terminate his lease? He had the feeling that God had a very important plan for him. Does God have such a plan for everyone that has lost a loved one? He thought probably not. After all, some people don't have as much trouble moving on in life as he had experienced. At the table he said, "Please God, answer my many questions before you expect me to leave."

Chapter Four

It was Saturday when Shane walked into the local sporting goods store. He knew the owner very well. They got to be friends when they worked together for a local landscaping business. Tom Watson, the owner of the store, greeted Shane as he walked in and they talked some about old times. The two of them had spent a couple of years playing on a softball team together. Tom knew how devastating it was for Shane when Becky had died. It had just taken the will out of Shane to go on. Tom was hoping that Shane was getting back to his old self. Shane told Tom that he was going on a long journey. He also told Tom that he would be walking.

That seemed kind of strange to Tom, so he said, "Where are you going?"

"I don't know," replied Shane.

Tom asked, "How long will you be gone?"

"I don't know," Shane replied again.

Tom asked if he was going with someone else and Shane replied, "No, I'll be going alone." Tom was concerned but he got everything for Shane that he wanted.

He walked out of the store with a quality backpack, a good lightweight tent, a wonderful sleeping bag, and the finest hiking boots that Tom had in the store. He then went to the supermarket and bought some food that would not spoil on him and would be good for hiking. He arrived home, packed up his backpack and got ready for the time when he would be leaving his South Carolina apartment.

He told the apartment management office that he would be leaving soon. A young lady in the office who had only been working there a short time asked if he would be interested in selling all of his furniture. She said she would be very interested in his apartment. It was arranged that when it was time for Shane to leave, he would notify her immediately. Shane told her he would be leaving in a hurry and knew it would be soon but he didn't know exactly when. Sally was pleased that she was getting an apartment right where she worked.

Shane paid all of his bills up-to-date. He was ready to go whenever God told him it was time to start the walk of his life. It was that very night when Shane was woken up around 2 a.m. God was sitting on the edge of his bed. God answered as many of Shane's questions as He could at the time. God said, "You will be leaving in the morning. After you have everything set with Sally, you will start walking west."

Shane wanted to know if he would be seeing God again. "You will, Shane. You will see me again. I won't appear to you every day but I will keep you safe on your journey," God replied.

Shane woke up around 7 a.m., called Sally and everything was squared away with her. Shane had plenty of money on him but he didn't want to carry all he had, so he had his ATM card with him. With the pack on his back, he said goodbye to Sally. They waved to each other as he was rounding the corner at the end of the street. Step after step, he continued for the first day stopping just before dark by a little stream that seemed out in the middle of nowhere. Shane was very tired and set up his tent and crawled into his sleeping bag much earlier than he would normally sleep. That first night, he slept like a log, not waking up once until he saw sunlight shining into the tent. He had a snack bar for breakfast and drank a little water.

Soon, it was time to start day two on the road. He was traveling along a back road when a man in a pickup truck stopped to ask if he wanted a lift. Shane politely turned him down saying, "Thank you for the offer but I'm really enjoying the hike." There was no way he was going to tell the man that God told him he had to walk. It was one of the rules laid down by God – no riding. By the end of the second day, Shane was just as tired as the first. He had Becky in his mind most of the time those first two days. He wondered if he could ever love someone else. At this point in his life, he didn't think so. God was looking down on Shane constantly those first two days knowing that the toughest things in life will bring the biggest rewards.

Chapter Five

Shane figured he was walking about four miles an hour for about eight hours each day. It was early on the eighth day when he had walked over two hundred miles that he left South Carolina and entered the state of Georgia. By the eighth day, walking was getting easier. He spent the first night in Georgia about twenty miles from the Georgia-South Carolina line. He got a little ways off of the highway into a wooded area and saw a little clearing next to a nice pond. Shane felt he needed a good bath so he stripped down and took a nice swim in the pond. *It is wonderful,* he thought. *This is the cleanest I have felt in days.*

He pitched his tent and climbed into his sleeping bag just as it was getting dark. Thinking was what Shane had been doing for days. He was wondering what he would find when he reached the end of his journey. It had been eight days – a long time to be walking when you don't even know where you are going. It was just starting to rain lightly when Shane closed his eyes for the night. The days were tiring and he had no trouble falling asleep.

Sometime during the night, his eyes opened to see God kneeling down beside him. "How are you doing, Shane?" God asked. Shane told God that it was tiring but rewarding. He had always liked to walk, but he wished he knew just where he was going. God said, "In due time, you will know." He had to wonder why God wouldn't tell him where he was going or how long it would take. He finished the night in a deep sleep and didn't wake up until almost 9 a.m. He was only a couple of miles from the first town he would come to in Georgia. He was hoping that he could stop somewhere in town and get a good breakfast.

Shane walked into town and came to Ann's Diner. He went inside and settled down in a booth. Shane always liked booths and didn't like sitting at a table or at the counter. A booth was always much more comfortable to him. A waitress came up to him and handed him a menu. She said, "Hi, stranger. Are you just passing through town?"

"Yes, I am but I wanted to have a good breakfast before I continue my journey," Shane said.

"Where are you going?" she wanted to know.

Shane had the same reply for everyone. "I don't know," he said. Shane was starting to feel bad saying that to everyone but to be honest, he really didn't know.

He took his time eating breakfast and having a couple of cups of coffee. He didn't want to leave the diner but he knew he had to get moving along. He thanked the waitress and handed her a nice tip as he stepped outside. He saw a little grocery store across the highway and went inside to pick up a few more things to eat as he traveled through Georgia. He was now on his way walking west again. Shane was crossing northern Georgia and he figured it would take him about six days.

Shane was meeting some wonderful people on the way through Georgia. He often stopped to talk with people for a little while. It slowed down his forward progress but he was once again feeling like life was worth living. Shane was sitting near a stream one night and started to think about life and what the future would hold. He realized now why God had wanted him to walk. He wanted Shane to mingle with people and to enjoy life. He would often stop and stare up into a tree to watch a little bird. He was now seeing the finer things in life. He was finally starting to realize that there was life after Becky. He looked up into the sky and said, "Thank you, God. I think I am starting to realize why you sent me on this journey."

It was on the fourteenth day, which seemed like such a long time since he took his first step of the journey, that he was getting ready to leave Georgia and step into the northeast corner of Alabama. He thought that no matter what God had planned, he was so glad that he was making this trip. He was now feeling better than he had in years. He had even been singing as he went about his merry way.

Chapter Six

Shane was just crossing the northeast corner of Alabama on his way to Tennessee. It would probably be no more than fifty or sixty miles. It was while he was walking across that corner of the state that he came to a little farmers market stand along the side of the highway. It was nearing the end of the day and he would be settling down soon. He purchased some fruit and put them into his backpack. Fresh fruit was going to be a special treat for him.

He got talking to the lady that ran the stand. She was so cheerful and wanted to know where Shane was headed.

"You probably won't understand but really, I don't know where I'll end up," he replied.

The young woman, Sylvia Chestnut, gave a smile and then asked, "Where are you staying for the night?"

Shane said that he would stop someplace along the highway and pitch a tent for the night. Sylvia wanted to know how long it had been since he had a home cooked meal.

Kind of sheepishly, Shane bowed his head and said, "Not since my wife died over three years ago."

"I don't usually do this but how would you like to come to my house and have a home cooked meal?" Sylvia asked.

Shane told her that he would be forever grateful for her kindness. Sylvia told Shane that she would be closing up the stand in a few minutes. With everything put away for the night, they started to walk to Sylvia's house which was located a short distance behind the stand.

As Sylvia was getting ready to prepare dinner, she asked Shane if he would like to have a shower. Shane told her that he had been walking for days and would love to clean up proper.

She showed him where the bathroom was and said, "There are towels in the cabinet."

The shower felt so good that Shane didn't want to get out of it. It felt like he could have stayed in there all night. He finally stepped out of the shower and dried off. He put on a clean pair of jeans that he had in his backpack.

Shane looked in the mirror and said, "I need to get rid of this beard." He shaved and felt his face. It felt so smooth and between the shower and the shaving, he felt like a new man. Shane noticed that from days of walking in the sun he was getting quite a tan. It did make him look more handsome. It was then that he thought, *I wonder how Becky would have liked my new rugged look.*

Shane made his way out to the kitchen and said, "Something smells real good in here."

Sylvia turned around and said, "Wow, look at you. You look so handsome." Shane's face turned a little red from the compliment. Sylvia said, "Dinner will be ready soon. You can either sit in the living room or stay out here and keep me company."

"I'd like to stay here and chat with you," Shane said. He hadn't had many people to talk to on the road, and it was a pleasure spending some time with Sylvia.

They had a wonderful dinner of roast chicken, mashed potatoes, corn on the cob, fresh baked rolls and blueberry pie for dessert. They talked as they had their meal. It was as much of a treat for Sylvia as it was for Shane. Sylvia's husband was killed in Iraq a few years ago. She told how much of a shock it was and how she cried for weeks. Sylvia asked Shane how hard it was when his wife was killed in the accident.

"I thought life was over for me. I've been struggling with her death for three years," said Shane. She wanted to know if his walking journey was a way for him to heal. He nodded his head as to say yes it is.

"What gave you the idea to walk hundreds of miles?" she asked.

Shane didn't know if he should tell her. "Sylvia, it was God that put me on this journey," he said. He didn't know if she would believe it or not.

"I understand, Shane. When my husband died, I was visited that very night by God. If He hadn't, I don't know if I would have made it through this."

They talked for the longest time that night. Shane hadn't felt that comfortable around a woman for a long time. Sylvia told Shane he could spend the night in the guest room. Shane told her it would be nice but he didn't want to inconvenience her.

She smiled and said, "It is nice to have a man in the house and someone to talk with. I get very lonesome at times."

Shane felt so good sleeping in a real bed that night. He didn't think anything could wake him up.

Chapter Seven

Shane woke up a little after 8 a.m. He took his time cleaning up before going into the kitchen. "Good morning, Sylvia," he said.

She turned around with a big smile on her face. She said, "Did you sleep well?" Shane told her it was such a treat to sleep in a real bed after being on the road for over two weeks. Sylvia said, "It was nice that you stayed. I'm glad you did."

"Sit down and I'll make you a good breakfast," she said. Shane was hungry and felt so good having a good meal last night and another one this morning. "I don't suppose I can talk you into staying for a while longer," she said.

Shane said he really would like to but he had to get back to walking. They sat at the table and had breakfast together. Sylvia so much enjoyed Shane's company and wished he could have stayed longer but she understood.

"If you ever get back this way, I hope you will stop in and see me," Sylvia said.

Shane told her that he surely would. It had been such a pleasure spending a little time with her. It brought Shane into the idea that he didn't have to keep to himself any longer. It was one of the most pleasurable times he had spent in a long time. He wasn't about to forget Becky, but Sylvia was a fine, kind, and caring woman. She showed Shane a lot of sweetness. Sylvia told Shane to wait a few minutes while she made a few sandwiches for him to take along. It was wonderful knowing that he would be having something good to eat that night.

He continued walking in northern Alabama knowing that sometime late that evening he would be entering Tennessee. Walking along, he took a drink of water, smiled and realized that he had met some wonderful people on this trip. He had taken in the pleasures of nature every step of the way. Often times, he would stop to see a bird flying overhead, a bird sitting on a tree branch singing a song to him, or watch a deer cross the highway. *This is why God wanted me to walk,* he thought. *He wanted me to get back to the basics of life. If I was driving, I never would have had as much joy on this trip as I have been having.*

It was just before dark when he saw the sign that he was entering Tennessee. *Tennessee, the land of country music,* he thought to himself. Shane walked off the highway for a little while when he came to a clearing where he would pitch his tent. The tent up and the sleeping bag rolled out, he sat on a rock and stared into the star-filled sky. He pulled one of the sandwiches out of his backpack that Sylvia had made for him. It was delicious ham and cheese, so good that Shane reached into his backpack and decided to have another one. They felt so good after a long day of walking. That left one more sandwich in his backpack that he would have tomorrow. He had been traveling a little more north for the past day but now that he was in Tennessee, he would be back to going west again.

He didn't crawl into his sleeping bag early that night. The moon was just coming up over the horizon and it made his first night in Tennessee magical. He was smiling and reflected back on his journey since he left South Carolina. The people who he had met had given him memories that he would remember for the rest of his life. There was a purpose for him being on this journey. God had given him a second chance at a good life. It took miles before he realized it, but for a man that seldom smiled after his wife Becky died, every minute of life was now enjoyable. He sat on a rock and looked up at the moon with tears in his eyes. They were happy tears. He looked up into the sky and said a few words, "Thank you, God."

Chapter Eight

Shane woke up early the next morning even though he didn't go to sleep until late. It was like his body was rejuvenated. He felt like a man ten years his junior. Ready to get on the road, he packed everything up. With the pack on his back, he walked back to the road and continued his journey west step after step. Shane kept a smile on his face that whole day and waved and talked to many people. All were interested in the story of what he had been doing the last few weeks.

Tennessee was a beautiful state to Shane. It was a nature lover's paradise. Walking across Tennessee took him over a week. Now over three weeks into his journey, what started out as something he didn't look forward to now became something he loved doing. He sat on the bank of the mighty Mississippi River and looked in awe. It was an amazing sight. He was thinking that there is a lot of history to that river.

He remembered back to when he was a youngster and read Mark Twain's classics, "Life on the Mississippi" and "The Adventures of Huckleberry Finn." How he loved those books and now years later, he was sitting on the bank of the Mississippi River and gazing out over the water. He closed his eyes and pictured Huckleberry Finn rafting down the river. It was an amazing experience for him, probably one of the most memorable of his life.

He spent that night on the river bank and woke up early the next morning. It was time for him to move on. He ate a snack bar that he had in his backpack. It would be enough for him until later in the day. Hoisting his backpack onto his back, he walked along the river bank until he came to the bridge that crossed the mighty Mississippi. Taking one last look from his vantage point, he said to himself, "*Get moving Shane, a long way to go today.*"

Shane crossed that bridge and came out the other end to enter the state of Arkansas. He had now traveled over six hundred and fifty miles. As he took that first step into another state, he wondered how many steps he had taken on his journey. Shane's look had become more weathered. His face, arms, and legs had a darkened tan. He now looked like a man that had seen much of life. What was surprising to Shane was how much he was enjoying life – thanks to Becky and God! Only a few short months ago, he never realized that he would be smiling so much.

Shane looked at his map and saw that Arkansas was going to take him a long time to cross. His first day was so enjoyable until early in the afternoon. The sky started to darken and there was no doubt that rain was on the way. He found a heavily wooded area a few hundred yards off of the highway next to a little stream. Washing up made him feel a lot better. Putting up his tent, he put everything inside to keep dry. It was only an hour later when the rains came. He took a paperback out of his backpack and spent the rest of the day reading. Just before dark, he had a light snack and said, "I would love to have one of Sylvia's ham and cheese sandwiches right now." Sylvia was a fine, kind, and attractive woman but Shane knew that wasn't where his journey was supposed to end.

It rained all through the night and into the next day. Shane thought that he probably wouldn't be doing any walking that day. He was right. It wasn't until after seven in the evening when the rain finally stopped. He did step out of his tent and walked around. It felt so good just to stretch.

After spending well over a day staying in his little tent, he was anxious to get back on the road, but it would have to wait until the next day.

Back in his tent, Shane settled down for the night. He didn't sleep well that night, probably because he kept thinking about the time his journey would end. What would he find? Would he be happy? Would he be scared? *No*, he thought. *God will keep me safe and lead me to the road that will put my life back on track.*

Chapter Nine

Shane had lost some time because of the long rain storm that had kept him in his tent. He really didn't mind because it gave him some time to rest his weary muscles. He did enjoy reading his paperback and listening to the rain pitter patter on his tent. In a way, it was very relaxing. However, he was glad to get back on the highway and continue his journey west.

He met a young couple taking a bicycle ride. They told Shane that they did it every morning. It was good exercise and got them out into the fresh air. Shane said, "I know what you mean. The fresh air is amazing."

They wanted to know how long Shane had been on the road and where he was going.

He said, "It's been well over a month now. I started close to the coast in South Carolina. I'm heading west but where my final destination is I don't know yet. I'll know when I get there." The young couple wished him well and continued their bike ride.

Shane covered a lot of ground that day. The weather was beautiful and it was a little cooler after the rain. A light breeze was in the air making a perfect day for walking. Shane talked to several other people before walking into a small town. He spotted a diner that looked fairly busy. He stepped inside and took a seat at the counter.

A little grey-haired woman came over to him and said, "Welcome stranger, can I get you something?" Thinking of

Sylvia, he ordered a ham and cheese sandwich with french fries and a sweet tea. Having snacks on the road is fine but it is a treat to walk into a diner and sit down with other people.

Several of the people next to him came over and asked about his trip. They could all see that it looked like he had been hiking for a long time.

One old man who appeared to be in his seventies asked, "Where do you sleep at night?"

"Usually I pitch my tent a distance off the highway and snuggle into my sleeping bag," Shane replied.

The old man admitted that he didn't have much room in his little home. He had a barn with a hay loft for his two horses. "I love horses," he said. He told Shane that he had always had a horse since he was a little boy. He let Shane know that he was welcome to spend the night in the hay loft. Shane gladly accepted the old man's kindness.

They finished up their meals and walked the short distance to the old man's home. Entering the barn, he saw two beautiful horses. Shane said, "My journey would be a lot quicker if I was riding one of these." They both laughed and chatted for a couple of hours.

Shane wanted to know if the old man was married. He said, "I was but my wife died of cancer a few years ago. It's been hard since she passed away. We were married forty-nine years and a few months. We were looking forward to our Golden anniversary." With tears in his eyes he said, "We didn't quite make it."

"I'm sorry," Shane said. He told the old man that he had lost his wife in a car accident a few years ago.

The old man told Shane how sorry he was to hear that. "You are a young man son. I'm sure you will get married again," he said. Shane nodded his head, yes. The old man said, "I better get to bed. Sleep well." Shane thanked him and he got down on the hay and was asleep almost as soon as his eyes closed.

Shane didn't wake up once during the night. It was a great night's sleep. He woke up early in the morning by the sound of a rooster. He sat up and smiled before saying, "I don't need an alarm clock here, do I?" He looked over at the horses who were staring back at him. All Shane could think of was the experiences he had been having. They were incredible experiences that would remain in his memory until the day he died.

The old man walked out to the barn and with a chuckle said, "That old rooster really can wake you up, can't he?" They both laughed and talked for a few minutes.

Shane said, "Before I start walking today, I'm going to the diner and have breakfast. To show my thanks for your hospitality, will you join me for breakfast?"

The old man nodded his head yes and off to the diner they walked. They got a booth in the corner by a window and ate and talked for over an hour. Finally, Shane said, "I have to get on the road. I have many miles to go on my journey." They walked back to the barn and with the backpack on his back, Shane shook the old man's hand and thanked him for his kindness.

The old man watched Shane walk away, until he was almost out of sight. Shane turned around and they both waved to each other. The old man walked back to his house with tears in his eyes. He whispered, "Good luck, Shane. I'll miss you."

Chapter Ten

Shane was having a good day and covering a lot of ground. Several people stopped and asked if he wanted a ride, but as usual, he turned them all down. It wasn't so much now that it was one of God's rules that he must walk, but he was enjoying it. He thought of how much he would have missed if he was driving himself or riding with someone else. Shane knew that the real way to see America was on foot.

It was well into the afternoon when he came to a large lake. It was a state park and had a beach. There was no way that Shane was going to pass up the chance to take a swim. He sat his backpack down in the sand and took off his shirt.

Several young girls of probably college age looked at him, giggled and asked if he was a mountain man.

He probably did look that way. His hair was getting long and he had quite a beard since the last time he shaved. He said, "No, I'm not a mountain man but maybe I do look that way. I've been walking since South Carolina and am enjoying my journey."

"Wow!" one of them said. "Tell us what it's been like."

"I will," he said. "But let me take a quick dip in the lake first."

The water felt so refreshing that he didn't want to get out of the lake. He went back and told the girls of his journey. They were so interested and one of them asked, "Were you ever scared?"

He replied, "Actually, no. Everyone has been so kind and pleasant." He told them of the night before when he had met an old man and slept in his barn. He even told them of the night Sylvia let him stay in her house. "I've had people give me food and it has been so much appreciated."

One of the girls asked how much longer he would be walking.

"I don't really know. I'll know when I get there," Shane said.

Shane stood up, put his shirt back on and lifted up his backpack. "It was nice talking to you girls but I have to get back to my journey."

All of them got up and gave Shane a hug and wished him good luck. One of the girls said, "I hope you find what you are looking for." They all told him how nice of a man he was.

Shane stepped away with a smile on his face. They were such nice, sweet and polite girls. *I just keep running into the finest people*, he thought.

It was a long stretch across Arkansas, but he enjoyed every step of it. The scenery was beautiful and the people were some of the nicest he had met on his journey. Step after step, mile after mile, he kept heading west. Shane thought, *I hope I don't have to walk all the way to California*. However, he had no idea how far he was going. Maybe California was a possibility. Time would tell when his journey would be over. He was enjoying himself and for now, that was the only thing that mattered. He still thought of Becky. Shane knew that he always would; however, it was changing from the sadness and depression that he lived through for years to more of smiles and great memories.

He had so many good memories of his life with Becky. Their vacations, their weekends together, their nights of cuddling on the sofa watching a good movie on TV would be in his memory forever. Shane smiled and wondered if he would ever meet someone that he loved as much as Becky. He was now sure he would, but he felt that the love may be different. Shane thought that if you love more than one woman in your life, you shouldn't or couldn't compare the two women. They would each have their own special traits that would cause you to love them.

Shane did a lot of thinking that day as he was walking along. He wondered why there was so much divorce. He didn't understand how two people could fall in love, get married, and then in a short time, get divorced. He wasn't against divorce because he knew it would be better than staying together and not being happy. The only thing that made Shane sad was that the children were often the ones that got hurt the worst. It often devastated them to see their parents split up. Spending time at one parent's place and then spending time at the other parent's had to be difficult for them.

Shane was now about halfway through Arkansas. It was one of the longest legs in his journey. He was spending about nine days getting across that state. Probably in about another four days or a little more, he would be leaving it and seeing a sign that would say "Leaving Arkansas," and then another one that would say "Welcome to Oklahoma." He smiled as he settled down for the night next to a little lake. With the tent up and his sleeping bag out, he took a little time to do some reading. He looked up at the stars and said, "Thank you God for sending me on this journey." It had been a pleasure meeting so many nice people. What would the following days have in store for him? He wished that he knew but was sure that it would be an adventure. He soon settled into his sleeping bag before another day on the road.

Chapter Eleven

It had been nice walking, as Shane was only a couple of days from the Oklahoma border. He wondered what Oklahoma was like. He had never been to that state, so this would be a new experience that he was looking forward to. It was around noon when he saw another hiker coming from the other direction. Jimmy Jackson was his name and he had also been on the road for quite some time. He had been hiking from Colorado and would eventually see the Atlantic Ocean – his dream.

"Shane have you ever wondered what it was like a couple of hundred years ago?" Jimmy said.

"I bet it was really wonderful and beautiful at that time. No hustle and bustle, just unspoiled natural beauty," replied Shane.

Jimmy nodded his head, yes. They chatted for a little bit, had a little snack and both then went their separate ways.

Shane enjoyed talking with people. It made every day easier and more enjoyable. He had never loved life any more than this, naturally except the time he had Becky. Becky had to be looking down on him as he was walking along and smiling. It was a warm day and Shane decided to take off his shirt. He had been drinking a lot of water. He just finished the bottle he was carrying and knew he would have to get more in the next town.

A car just passed when he saw out of the corner of his eye a dog run across the highway. The car swerved in an attempt to miss it and ran head on into a utility pole. The front of the car was smashed in severely. Shane ran as fast as he could to the car. There was a little baby in the back seat. He got her out and took her to safety. Running back to the car, he saw flames from underneath. Yanking the door open, he saw the woman was badly hurt. He cut off her seatbelt and gently, with ease pulled her out of the car. He pulled her over to where he had laid her baby. Another car with a middle-aged couple arrived on the scene and Shane asked them to call the police and an ambulance.

Just then, the car exploded with an incredible bang. Shane laid his body across the woman and the baby. A few pieces of debris landed very close to them. The baby appeared in good shape but the woman was bleeding severely. Shane applied first aid and got the bleeding to stop just as the ambulance arrived, followed by the police a few minutes later. The paramedics praised Shane, telling him he had done a great job. Shane had a couple of cuts on his right arm that they took care of. The ambulance pulled away. Then the police asked Shane a lot of questions. The one officer said, "That woman is lucky you were right here or she and her baby would have probably been burned alive in that car." Shane shuddered at the thought of dying that way.

After the police left, Shane walked a little distance and came upon a stream along the side of the road. He sat down and cried and cried. It brought back a flood of memories of Becky dying in a car accident. He had never personally seen a car accident before and it scared the daylights out of him, but he jumped into action immediately. He was so glad that he was there to help. If he hadn't been, they would surely have died. He had been walking a long time and this was the darkest time of his journey. Was this accident in the plans laid out for him? Was this a test by God? If it was, he knew that he had passed. The accident really shook him up and he needed to rest. He followed the stream back into the forest for a short distance. Shane always felt better getting away from the sight of the highway before he pitched his tent. He felt a lot safer being out of everyone's sight.

It was still only about 6 p.m. – a long time yet before it would be dark. He sat on a rock near the stream and just thought back on the day. It started out so peacefully and ended up with a scare. He knew though that the woman and little baby would be fine. *Why couldn't someone have been there for Becky?* he thought. That is a question that he would never have an answer for. Shane couldn't eat anything that night. He was too upset. A lot of thoughts went through his mind that night. He looked up and saw the sky. Staring at the stars brought him some peace for the day.

He got in his sleeping bag and stayed awake for the longest time. Sleep took a long time to come that night. Once he did get to sleep, he didn't wake up until the sun was high in the sky. He unzipped his tent to see God standing a short distance away. God said, "Shane, you did an incredible job yesterday saving two people's lives. You should feel very proud."

"Was this planned for me? Was it a test?" Shane asked.

"No Shane, it was purely a coincidence. I needed to tell you that you are a wonderful man and Becky is so proud of you," God said.

As God's presence was fading away, Shane said, "Thank you, God. Thank you." Tears were running down Shane's cheeks and dropping to the ground. The words that God just said to him would be a lifelong memory.

Chapter Twelve

Shane was soon walking along the highway heading west. It looked like it was going to be another warm day. He had filled up his water bottle from the stream that he camped beside. He didn't want anything to eat for the longest time. Shane was still very upset from the day before. It was something that he would not easily forget. Probably because it reminded him so much of Becky, he would never forget.

Shane soon came to a small town and walked through it, saying hello to everyone. *This is a nice town*, he thought. *Everyone is so kind.* He noticed a little ice cream stand on the one corner. He took a couple of dollars out of his pocket and bought himself a vanilla cone. It really hit the spot for Shane.

He sat on a little bench finishing his cone when a little boy came up to him and said, "Where are you walking to mister?"

Shane smiled at him and said, "I'm not sure, but I have been walking for a long time now – well over a month."

"Why don't you drive?" the little boy said.

Shane chuckled and said, "I have my reasons." Finishing his cone, he got up and put his backpack on, saying to the boy, "Would you like an ice cream?"

The boy smiled and said, "Oh yes, thank you mister." Shane handed the boy some money for an ice cream and then continued on his walk.

Step after step, he continued. He had no idea how many steps he had taken. Shane really would have liked to know. He knew it had to be a lot to wear down the soles on his shoes the way he had. He had purchased a couple of bottles of water before he left the town. He also wondered how many bottles of water he had since starting out on the journey. Many thoughts now appeared to be coming to Shane. It was just about dark when he saw the sign in the distance that he knew he would probably see that day. He was now leaving Arkansas and walked up to the sign: "Welcome to Oklahoma." He ran his hand across the sign as people were driving by in their cars.

This was a major accomplishment in his trip. For some reason – and he didn't know why – he felt that the end of his journey was approaching. Shane had that feeling, but it wasn't to be. He still had a long journey ahead of him. By the time he got to the end, he would be glad that it was over in a way but in many ways, he wouldn't. Shane walked just a little into Oklahoma and went off the highway for a few hundred yards before finding a nice spot to pitch his tent. He was tired that night but he thought of the little boy. It made him smile and kind of laugh. He wondered if he would ever have a little boy of his own. He would love to have a son to go camping and fishing with.

He slept late again the next morning. It seemed like it had been happening a lot lately. However, he did cover a lot of ground once he got back to walking again. He didn't talk to anyone that day, so he covered a lot of miles. The next couple of days were like that. It did take up a lot of his time when he stopped to talk to people, but it brought him so much enjoyment. Shane had been keeping some notes on his journey. Would it make a good book, he wondered? He smiled and said, "If I sell one to everyone I know, at least I'll make a couple of bucks."

It was another week when he had a dream that he was supposed to start walking north. Why the change in direction, he wondered? When he came to a small town in northern Oklahoma about half the distance from east to west, a light appeared to him in the sky. He knew this was where he was supposed to start walking north. He said, "I hope I don't have to walk all the way to Canada." He didn't know it yet, but he had a couple of more days to spend in Oklahoma. They were good days. He got to meet some really nice people.

All totaled, by the time he reached the Oklahoma-Kansas border, he spent 16 days in Oklahoma alone. He woke up his first morning in Kansas with a strange feeling. *Is there something about Kansas that I should know?* he thought.

Chapter Thirteen

Shane walked north for a few days in Kansas. The land seemed so flat but the people were so friendly. His second night, he met an older couple in a diner. They got to talking and enjoyed hearing so much about Shane's travels. It was almost two hours before they left the diner. The older couple asked if he would like a nice bed to sleep in that night. He said, "I'd love to, but do you live far away?"

They told him they lived only about a quarter of a mile away. Shane said, "I can't tell you why but I have to walk there." They looked a little concerned but gave him directions to their house.

They were waiting on the front porch when Shane walked up to the house. "Come on inside," the old man said.

"It is a nice house you have here," Shane said. They talked for the longest time. He found out that they had been married for fifty-three years. *Wow, that is a long time*, Shane thought to himself. Shane kept looking at them and they seemed so happy. They were both in their late seventies and sharp as a whip.

It was near midnight when they showed Shane to their guest room. "Sleep well," they said. Shane felt so good in a real bed again. He hadn't had a real bed to sleep in since he spent the night at Sylvia's house. Shane wondered how she was. He hoped she was doing well and was sure she was. Shane woke up early and cleaned up and shaved. It made him feel so good. He sat down to put his hiking boots on and felt the bed move. Startled, he looked to his right and saw God sitting on the bed with him.

God said, "I'm glad you are well rested and that you cleaned up and shaved. You will not hear from me again, Shane. You will enter a small town of Change, Kansas. That is where your journey will end."

"What will I find there?" Shane asked.

"There is no need for me to tell you. You will know," God replied.

God faded away as Shane sat on the bed wondering. He went downstairs to see the older woman in the kitchen and the man having a cup of coffee. Turning around, they wanted to know how Shane slept. "I slept great last night. It was so nice sleeping in a real bed," he said.

"Sit down, son, and I'll make you some breakfast," the old woman said. It was delicious –pancakes, eggs, bacon, and toast.

He asked them one question before he left: "How far is it to Change?"

"Only about eighteen miles," the old man said. Shane thanked them so much for their kindness as he stepped off of their front porch and made his way to the highway.

It was early afternoon when he entered the town of Change, Kansas. It was so clean. Shane didn't see any litter anywhere. People waved at him and shouted hello. There was a little park in the center of town with nice shade trees and park benches throughout. Shane went to one of those benches and sat down. He pulled out an apple from his backpack and ate that while he was waiting for what he didn't know to happen. Shane was curious as to what God meant when he told Shane that he would know when it happens.

Shane sat on the bench for about an hour and a half when a young woman walked up to him and said, "Do you mind if I sit down with you?"

"Please join me," Shane said. She introduced herself and told Shane her name was Gina Albertson.

"I've been walking for months from near the coast of Oregon," she said. Gina was a gorgeous woman – slender build, a smile that could light up a room – and she had the most pleasant personality Shane had ever seen. Her long brown hair was hanging down past her shoulders. Gina said, "Shane, I think we need to talk."

"I know we do," he said.

Chapter Fourteen

Shane looked around and saw a little outside café across the street. Shane said, "Would you like to go over to that café and have something? We could talk there."

"That would be nice, Shane," Gina replied. Shane reached out and took ahold of her hand to help her up. As their hands touched, something came over them. It was amazing – as if their bodies had entered a different dimension. They both felt so peaceful. They were in a field. They were walking through the tall grass. They saw nothing of the little city park they were standing in.

It was as if the park had never existed. They were just walking hand in hand in a different dimension. Where were they really? What had overcome them? It was a sign from above that they would be spending much time together. They were meant for each other. If they weren't, God would never have arranged for this meeting to take place. It seemed like they were spending a whole day in total peace.

Gina had stood up but they were still hand in hand. They looked around and there was no sight of the city park. They weren't even thinking of it. It was like it didn't exist. Shane and Gina didn't have a care in the world. All either one could think of was the other. At that point in time, nothing else around them existed. Other people were walking around the park and many of them were staring at Shane and Gina.

People were seeing them standing there, holding hands. They were looking into each other's eyes but they were not talking – just standing there. Several people came up to them and asked, "Are you alright?" Neither Shane nor Gina looked at them or said anything. It was an amazing sight to see. People could see them both enveloped in a soft mist. Shane and Gina were both smiling as they held each other's hand. What was God telling them? They had both been through tough times in the last few years.

The mist was clearing away from Shane and Gina. They both shook their heads and in unison said to each other, "Did you feel that? What was it?" They both shook their heads in disbelief. Neither one had ever felt anything like it. Shane had glanced at his watch when he got up from the bench. It was 2:45. He glanced at his watch again and it was 6:20 – over three and a half hours that couldn't be explained. Shane and Gina were both in awe. Something was mysterious here – unexplained.

Shane said, "Let's go to the café, Gina."

"Yes Shane, now we have more than ever to talk about. I have never felt anything like that in my life," Gina said. Shane agreed. It was amazing, incredible, and peaceful. They walked across the street to the café. They placed an order and then went outside to take a table on the beautiful day. Soon, the food arrived and they both started to open up about what was taking place. Shane told Gina about the time he was so depressed when his wife Becky was killed. It was over three years when God came and sent him on this journey. It had been well over fourteen hundred miles. Shane then filled in all of the details to Gina about what the last few months had been like.

Gina just sat there and took it all in. In amazement, she was about to tell Shane the story of her life the last few years. How could two people go through such heartache and then be sent on such identical journeys?

Chapter Fifteen

It was now Gina's turn to tell her story. She said, "I got into a very bad marriage a few years ago." She told of how Terry seemed like such a gentleman while they were seeing each other. Terry was a tall handsome man whom all of the young women swooned over. They dated a year and everything seemed so wonderful. Terry proposed and they set the wedding date for the following summer. From first appearances, it looked like a match made in heaven. The wedding ceremony was gorgeous and the honeymoon in Bermuda was more beautiful than she ever hoped for.

The first month or so went fine and then Terry started to just leave the house in the early evening and didn't come home until late. He would always come home drunk. Naturally, Gina told Shane that she objected but Terry wouldn't listen. Terry often belittled Gina in front of other people, especially Gina's friends. Often crying herself to sleep at night, she would be asleep before Terry came stumbling in.

After about the first year of marriage, Terry was becoming extremely abusive – both emotionally and physically. Often, she would have bruises all over her body and she was afraid to leave the house. She was feeling like a prisoner and that there was no escape for her. In the four years of their marriage, most of it was a living hell. Gina thought that often listening to Terry tell her she was no good, useless, and would never amount to anything was worse than the beatings.

Numerous times in the four years, the police were often called to the house by neighbors who feared for Gina's life. Gina would never file charges. She was afraid that when Terry got out of jail, he would kill her. There was no doubt in her mind that she was not going to live much longer. The emotional abuse and beatings were endless. It was happening so often that it finally became an every night thing. She hated Terry with a passion and was often forced to have sex while he was totally and disgustingly drunk.

It was near the end of the fourth year of marriage that Gina decided enough was enough. She bought a hand gun and took lessons on how to use it during the day, while Terry was at work. Gina kept it hidden underneath the bed. Terry came home very late one night in a terrible rage. Gina didn't know what caused it, but she felt this was the time that Terry was going to kill her. He beat her continuously almost from the time he stumbled through the front door. Gina was now battered and bruised. Terry had broken her left arm; she was bleeding badly. Gina was on the floor by the bed and Terry was coming after her with a baseball bat.

She was shaking violently, but slipped her hand under the bed and pulled out the hand gun. Pointing it at Terry, she said, "You won't ever beat anyone again, you rotten bastard." He smiled and raised the bat, getting ready to strike a killing blow. Gina pulled the trigger as Terry fell backwards. The final five shots went into Terry's chest. He lay dead near the bedroom door as Gina reached for the phone and called 911. The police and ambulance arrived in a few minutes but it seemed like hours.

There were no charges against Gina. It was clearly self-defense. Gina remained in the hospital for several days. She was then able to go home. She said, "I will never trust another man again." A few years went by and if Gina saw a man approaching her, she would run. If a man knocked on her door, she wouldn't answer it. Gina never left the house at night. She was in fear of any man after Terry's death for the next four years. Gina cried herself to sleep almost every night. She felt she would never have a normal life again.

Gina did have a job working in a nearby grocery store. She didn't want to become friends with anyone. Staying pretty much to herself, she did a good job; however, she just came in, did her job, and left at quitting time. Some people thought she was strange, but they didn't know what had happened to such a young woman. Gina said, "It was horrible, Shane. No one should ever have to go through what I did for four years."

"It is horrible and I'm sorry, Gina, but you have to believe that all men aren't like that," Shane said.

Chapter Sixteen

Gina continued telling her story to Shane. Gina said, "My husband was a monster and I really hated him, but I killed a man. Do you have any idea what that is like?"

"No, Gina, I have no idea. It must be a horrible feeling," Shane said.

Gina nodded her head before saying, "It is horrible to kill someone. The only thing I'm happy about is that he will never hurt anyone again." Shane gave Gina a hug and there was such a feeling of love between the two of them. It was as if someone had lit a candle on both ends and they would soon meet in the middle.

Gina told of how she was so scared of any man for years after she killed Terry. Because of the emotional abuse, she thought that every man acted like he did. Her depression got so bad that she considered suicide. It was on one of her worst mornings that when she woke up, God was sitting on her bed. God had said to her, "Gina, you have a long life to live yet." He told her of how He was planning a journey for her. Gina wanted to know more but God only said, "I will tell you more when the time is right."

Gina had no idea what He had meant. For several days, there was no more communication and Gina thought she was going crazy – after all, a visit from God? God appeared again late one night and said to Gina, "I want you to get a backpack, a small tent, a sleeping bag, some good hiking shoes, and some food supplies that won't spoil. It will be soon that I will tell you more about your journey." Gina got all of the supplies just like Shane had done. God appeared in a couple of more days and told Gina she would be walking southeast. He didn't tell her how far she would be going but did say it would be a long journey.

When it became time, she took that first step with many more to follow. She had no idea why she was walking, but she did find some nice, kind and interesting people along the way. For years, she had no idea that people could be so nice. As time went on, she was opening up to people and a smile that hadn't crossed her face in many years was now coming back to her. She was staying in a hotel one night after camping out for weeks. She looked in the bathroom mirror and saw a woman that she liked staring back at her. She had a smile on her face and realized she really was a beautiful woman.

That one night in the hotel made her feel better about herself. She had the feeling that God was with her every step of her journey. She knew that God was keeping the evil away and was only allowing her to be touched by kind, nice, caring, and wonderful people. She told Shane of one night when an older couple allowed her to stay in their home. Complete strangers showing her such kindness was something she had never felt before. It was a life-changing experience. Gina left that old couple's home the next morning with a smile on her face and tears in her eyes.

Gina kept telling Shane of her journey across America. As with Shane, it put her life back on track. She couldn't now believe that she was within days of ending her life. A few small prayers to God brought Him to her. It changed her life in a way that she would be forever thankful. She said, "Shane, I had no idea when I started my journey that God's plan was to put us together in the center of America."

Shane smiled and replied, "I had no idea either, Gina. It was a mystery to me. However, there is no doubt that the plan was to put us together." Shane told her how glad he was that he met Gina. Gina agreed and it was amazing how they felt about each other at first sight.

Shane had felt that he could never love anyone after Becky's death. Gina felt that she would never love any man after the years of abuse from Terry. Their long journeys and finding each other had put different feelings into their hearts and minds.

It was dark and they were still sitting at the table outside of the little café. The café would remain open for a few more hours. Shane got them both something to eat and drink. Gina said, "Where shall we stay tonight?"

"Why don't we get a couple of rooms at the hotel?"

They looked across the park and saw a nice hotel facing them. Gina said, "That's a good idea. Separate rooms are fine – at least until we get to know each other better." Shane agreed with Gina. They made their way across the park and entered the hotel. They each got their own room. Shane walked Gina to her room first and gave her a hug goodnight.

"Sleep well, Gina. I'll see you in the morning," he said.

She smiled and replied, "I wish it was morning already. You are a nice man, Shane Donaldson."

Shane walked to his room and entered. He took off his backpack and just stared at it for a few minutes. Shane knew that it was going to be time to retire the backpack and settle down. Shane wondered if Gina would want to live in Change, Kansas. It would be something to talk about in the morning. He was tired from a long day but was so happy that the journey was over. It was near fifteen hundred miles from start to finish. Shane looked at TV for a few minutes and then was so tired that he cleaned up and went to bed. He smiled and said, "Thank you, God." Shane closed his eyes and slept the whole night through without waking up once.

Chapter Seventeen

Shane and Gina remained in separate rooms in the hotel in Change, Kansas for a couple of days. They were sitting at a local diner one morning and Shane said, "We can't afford to stay in the hotel much longer."

Gina agreed but was uncertain about what they should do. Gina said, "You are a terrific man, Shane; however, I can't move in with any man right away. Call me old fashioned if you want but I feel we need to spend much time dating first."

"I understand," Shane said. They discussed it and realized that if they each got their own apartment it would cost more money and they wanted to save money.

After much discussion, they decided to get a two bedroom apartment. Gina said, "Ok, Shane, but you realize there will be no sex for a long time – no matter how much you beg."

Shane smiled and said, "It will be hard living with such a sweet, kind, and beautiful woman and not be tempted." Shane knew Gina was serious and after only a few days together, he could see that he wanted Gina in his life forever. Gina was just as much falling in love with Shane, but she had to be sure that she was making the right choice. Terry had really given her a fear of marriage.

They both got jobs – Shane working at a landscaping business and Gina as a waitress at the diner they liked going to. They got a two bedroom apartment just like they had planned. It gave them much time together and the love started to grow. The weekends were heaven because they could spend so much time together. There was no doubt that Shane was in love. Gina loved Shane, but she had so many horrible memories of the abuse that Terry gave her. It would take her longer, but there was no doubt that the couple would eventually wed.

Six months passed and Shane took Gina out to dinner one night. They took a walk in the park after dinner and sat on the bench where they first met. Shane said, "Do you remember the day we met on this bench?"

"Yes, I remember Shane. There is no doubt that day changed both of our lives."

Shane got down on one knee and said, "I love you, Gina. Will you marry me?"

Gina had tears in her eyes as she said, "Yes, oh yes." Shane slipped the ring on her finger and gave her a kiss that was so passionate. Gina couldn't get over how it felt to really be loved.

They sat on the park bench until almost midnight. Shane looked up at the stars and said, "Did you look at the stars often as you were on your journey?"

"Many times I looked at the stars and thought to myself: *why am I walking so far?*" Gina said. "I wondered if there was going to be something worthwhile when I took the last step of the journey."

"Well, are you happy with what you found?" Shane asked.

Gina hit Shane on the shoulder and said, "You know I am, Shane. I've never been happier."

They both smiled and Shane said, "I guess we better get back to our apartment. Tomorrow morning will be here soon."

Gina went to work at the diner the next morning and Sally, another one of the waitresses, screamed and pointed at

Gina's ring. All of the other help came around and gave her a big hug. Gina said, "Last night, Shane asked me to marry him." Some wanted to know when the wedding would be and she told them that they hadn't set a date yet.

Shane and Gina talked about that a lot and it seemed that it was already in their hearts what it would be. Their wedding would be on the same day that they first met in the park. It would be exactly one year from the time they met on the park bench. Gina said, "Shane, let's have the ceremony in the park."

Shane looked at Gina, smiled and said, "That is a fabulous idea." They had met many friends in only the six months that they had lived in Change, Kansas.

"I love this town. People are friendly and I want to live here the rest of my life," Gina said.

Shane added, "I love it here. It is a wonderful town and a great place to settle down."

They talked about what life would be like after they got married. Both of them had the dream of buying their own house and raising a family. And, both wanted a little dog. Gina knew that she had never been happier in her life. Shane was very happy once but he lost it when Becky died. They were now moving toward a life together – something they both wanted. Dreams were filling their heads of what they wanted it to be like.

The date was set for the wedding. Joe Carson, the owner of the diner, pulled Gina aside one morning and said, "Gina, would you like to have the wedding reception here in the diner? It will cost you and Shane nothing. All of the decorations and food will be provided by me. On the day of the wedding, I'll close the diner early."

Tears welled up in Gina's eyes. "Oh, thank you Joe. You are so kind. Shane and I accept your generous offer," she said. Gina gave Joe a huge hug and was so overcome by his kindness. Gina liked Joe. He was an amazing man.

When Gina got home, she told Shane of Joe's offer. They both hugged and loved the way everything was coming together. Life was fabulous. Neither one of them had been this happy in a lot of years. Shane would never forget Becky – and he shouldn't – but Gina was now in his life. He looked up in the sky and said, "Thank you, Becky. I love you." It was strange – Shane lost a woman he loved and Gina killed a man she hated. What did God see in the two of them that made Him want to bring them together? Whatever it was, Shane and Gina were so thankful.

Chapter Eighteen

Shane and Gina talked a lot of the time about what they wanted the wedding to be like. They were both simple people and did not believe in fancy affairs. It was quite a long time and after much discussion before they made their final decision. Shane said one morning, "Gina, how would you feel about having the wedding in the park in front of the bench where we first met?"

Gina smiled and said, "I think it is a wonderful idea! There couldn't be a better spot."

They were sitting at the table in their apartment sipping on their cups of coffee when Gina jumped up and said, "I have it, Shane! I have it!" Shane looked at her and smiled but wanted to know what she was so happy about. Gina said, "I don't want a wedding dress and I'm sure you don't want to dress up either." Shane looked at her and wondered what she was getting at. Gina continued, "Why don't we wear the same things that we were wearing when we first met in the park – backpacks and all. You can be sitting on the bench and I can walk up to you just like I did on that day."

"Honey, I think that is a fabulous idea," Shane said.

It was set in their hearts. Exactly one year after they first met, they would be married in the park. Gina told Joe when the wedding would be. "That's great!" Joe said. He asked Gina if she wanted to sit down with him after work and go over just how she wanted it to be. She told Joe that it would be great. She had so many things to discuss. Joe said,

"We're closing this diner and having a wonderful celebration." After work, the discussion began. Gina and Joe exchanged ideas and the plans were coming together. Joe wanted to make everything perfect for Gina and Shane.

Joe wanted to know how many people Gina and Shane would be expecting. "We want it to be a small wedding. We are planning on inviting our closest friends only," Gina said. "We are going to limit it to twenty-five people."

"That will be fine. I can remove the tables and chairs from the far corner of the diner. That will make a nice dance floor, don't you think?" asked Joe. Gina agreed that would be lovely. Joe didn't have to do it, but he told Gina he could get a local band to play at the wedding. Gina was so thankful for Joe's kindness.

Joe then said, "We can set up a buffet line along the counter and then there will be plenty of available seating at the booths and a few tables in the middle." Gina was so impressed with Joe's way of thinking. Joe then asked for a couple of stories about their journeys. Gina didn't know why, but Joe had some ideas in the back of his mind.

Shane planned on asking Bill, the owner of the landscaping business, to be his best man. *Bill would be glad to do it*, he thought. Gina said, "Shane, I know Joe is doing so much for us, but do you think he would give me away at the wedding?"

Shane smiled and said, "I'm sure he would, Gina. He thinks the world of you. After all, he treats you like a daughter." Gina didn't know it, but Joe lost his daughter to cancer nearly six years ago.

When Gina asked Joe if he would give her away, he broke out in tears. Gina said, "What's wrong Joe? I didn't mean to upset you."

Joe was a tough man who rarely showed emotion, but it overtook him like a thunderbolt that day. Joe said, "You don't understand, Gina. I will be honored to give you away.

It's just that I lost my daughter to cancer on what will be six years on your wedding day."

Gina gasped, not knowing what to say. Finally, she said, "I'm so sorry, Joe. I didn't know."

Joe told her that in a way, it would be like giving away his own daughter. Gina now understood why Joe treated her the way he did. Gina so much reminded him of his daughter, Sara. If Sara had lived, she would be just about Gina's age. It seemed like God had Joe in the plans this whole time. He was looking down on Joe, knowing that Joe needed this to ease the pain he had been having for the last six years.

Meanwhile, Shane asked Bill, "Would you be my best man at our wedding."

"You bet I will, Shane," answered Bill. "You are getting a fine woman in Gina." Bill knew that Shane and Gina were meant for each other. What he didn't know was that this whole process of the two meeting and leading up to the wedding was arranged by God. Bill had liked having Shane as a worker. Shane was never afraid of work and always put in the extra effort, which Bill very much appreciated. After all, when Shane makes a customer happy, then it makes the customer feel like he made a good choice in contacting Bill. He wanted to know where they were going on their honeymoon.

"Probably nowhere. We are trying to save money so we can eventually buy a house of our own," Shane said.

Bill looked at Shane and said, "You and Gina are two of the finest people I have ever known. You can't spend your honeymoon in Change, Kansas. I have some connections in the travel industry. How would you like to spend your honeymoon in Hawaii?"

"Bill, we don't have the money to do that," Shane said.

Bill replied, "The flight, hotel, rental car, and meals will all be on me. All you need is your own spending money." Shane was overcome by Bill's offer. He told Bill that it was just too much for him to accept. It seemed like the tears were flowing that day. Shane couldn't hold them back.

Bill told Shane that he would make the arrangements and let him know in the next few days. Joe and Bill had the plans to give them more than they ever hoped for. Gina and Shane each went home that day and told the other what was being planned. They were both shocked. They had never been so happy in their lives. Gina said, "Joe and Bill are two of the kindest people that we could ever hope to know."

Shane agreed that they were amazing and it had been a wonderful day. After dinner that night, they both snuggled up on the sofa and fell asleep in each other's arms.

Chapter Nineteen

The wedding day had arrived for Shane and Gina. It was a beautiful day in the park. There was an abundance of sunshine and a cool breeze was making it feel so refreshing. The grass was so green that it looked like it was a movie setting. Friends were gathering about and sitting on the lush grass in front of the bench where Shane and Gina had first met. Shane came walking from the sidewalk into the park with his backpack on. He approached the bench, took off his backpack and leaned it against the bench.

Soon, Reverend Tillman arrived and greeted Shane. The reverend thanked Shane for everything that Shane and Gina had been doing at the church. It was a quaint little church with everyone being so friendly. Shane and Gina had felt so welcome ever since the day that they first walked into Change, Kansas. The wedding was starting as the CD player sitting in the grass was playing the wedding march. Everyone turned around to see Joe proudly walking with Gina on his arm across the beautiful park grass. Joe felt so happy. He never got to give away his daughter Sara, but he was now giving away a very important woman in his life. Joe felt that Gina was like a daughter to him. Joe and Gina approached Shane, who was standing by the bench with the reverend and Shane's best man Bill.

Joe turned to Shane with a smile and said, "Take good care of this woman, Shane."

Shane smiled and replied, "I will. I love her very much."

Joe smiled and walked away with tears in his eyes. He was so happy for Shane and Gina. Reverend Tillman said a few words and then asked Shane if he wanted to say his vows. Shane turned to Gina taking her hand in his and said, "There was a time in my life when I thought it was over. Sitting on this very bench next to us exactly one year ago today, you walked into my life. We have spent a year getting to know each other. You have made me happy every day of it. I cherish you with all my heart. I promise you, Gina that I will do everything in my power to make you happy. I promise you that until death do us part you will be the most important thing in my life."

Reverend Tillman then asked Gina if she wanted to speak. Smiling, Gina said, "Over one year ago I started on a journey. It happened after I had endured years with an abusive husband. That came to an end one night when I shot and killed him. I was fearful of every man after that. God came to me and sent me on a journey that lasted months. I had no idea that when I approached this bench where you were sitting exactly one year ago that my journey was over. Actually, it wasn't over – for it has continued. You are part of my journey of life. I love you, Shane Donaldson and I want to spend the rest of my life with you. I promise you that I will forever love you like you deserve to be loved."

Reverend Tillman said, "Thank you, Shane and Gina, for your loving and sincere words." He continued with the ceremony and ended with the words, "You may kiss the bride." Shane kissed Gina for the longest time until everyone thought that it would never end. They were so happy. Reverend Tillman said to everyone sitting on the grass, "I present to you Mr. and Mrs. Shane Donaldson." In the usual casual style of the wedding, everyone clapped and cheered.

Everyone mingled in the park for quite some time. They all shook Shane's hand and congratulated him. The women all gave Shane a kiss on the cheek. Gina was being hugged by everyone and they all wished her a happy life. Everyone in attendance knew that this was a marriage that would last forever. They could just feel it. They knew that God had put them together. Shane and Gina had both spoken to God. When they started their journeys, neither one of them knew how theirs would end. They stood on the grass in the park close to the bench where they met. Holding hands and looking up into the clear blue sky, they said in unison, "Thank you, God. You have saved two very happy people."

It was time to head for Joe's diner. Joe and everyone else were there when Shane and Gina walked through the door. They all cheered, putting smiles on both of their faces. Shane and Gina looked over in the one corner where the band was going to play and saw a small tent set up with supplies lying about. There was a black covering fastened to the ceiling above the tent and stars were painted on the cover. Joe had made a little sign and placed it by the tent. On it was written, "Our journeys were worth every step." Gina started to cry; she was so happy. She couldn't believe how Joe had done so much for her. Joe was now placing the food out on the counter. He had slices of roast beef, slices of turkey, mashed potatoes, green beans, applesauce, carrots, peas, sweet rolls, soda, coffee, and tea.

Joe said, "Ok everyone, come and get it." The line moved along as people loaded their plates up with food. They sat at booths and tables and finished their meals. Everyone was complimenting Joe on how good the food was. Joe was smiling and was so happy. It was like his daughter was the one that was just married. As the meal came to an end, Joe brought out several blueberry pies. He said, "Not so quick everyone. Have some dessert." Naturally, everyone got a piece of Joe's pie. It was so delicious.

After dessert, Bill got up to say a few words. Bill said, "I was so happy to be asked to be Shane's best man. Shane isn't just one of my employees but a very good friend. When

I met Gina, I knew in my heart that someday they would be married. They are the perfect couple. I wish Shane and Gina years of happiness together." He lifted his glass as did everyone in attendance before saying, "God bless the two of you." After the toast, it was time to open some presents.

They got many things that they needed to make their apartment more like a home. Kitchen appliances, some wall hangings and small furniture were given to them. The final gift was a present that Bill handed to them in a brown envelope. Inside was the flight, hotel, car reservations and some money they would need for meals while they took their honeymoon to Hawaii. Shane and Gina were so thankful for all of the gifts and especially to Joe and Bill for their amazing kindness.

The band started to play, and called onto the dance floor were Mr. and Mrs. Shane Donaldson for their first dance as husband and wife. With the first dance in, everyone else was going onto the dance floor. What a wonderful day it had been. It was more than Shane and Gina ever would have imagined.

Chapter Twenty

Shane and Gina arrived at the airport in Wichita in the first step on their honeymoon to Hawaii. The first leg of their trip was from Wichita to Denver – not a really long flight. Neither Shane nor Gina had ever flown before. Both of them were a little nervous as they entered the plane, and the jitters increased as the plane rolled down the runway and lifted off into the clear blue sky above Wichita, Kansas. As they settled back into their seats, Gina said to Shane, "That wasn't bad, was it?" Shane just looked at her and smiled. Within a couple of hours, they would be landing at the airport in Denver.

With the first leg of their journey over, they waited in the Denver airport until it was time to board the next aircraft. This would be a seven and one-half hour flight from Denver to Honolulu. Shane and Gina talked much during that long stretch of time in the air. Gina told Shane how she had never been happier. Her marriage to Terry had taken a terrible toll on her and it climaxed when she shot Terry to death. Even though he was a monster, killing someone was something that she never imagined she could do. Shane took Gina's hand in his and said, "Don't worry, honey. I love you."

These were three little words she never heard Terry say. "I love you" was never in his vocabulary. It seemed like she had heard it so many times from Shane. Gina smiled, settled back in her seat and dozed off. Shane looked over at her and smiled as well. He was happier than he had been in years.

After a few hours, Gina woke up and looked over at Shane. Now he was fast asleep. It gave Gina a little bit of a chuckle. "What are we going to do, spend the whole flight sleeping?" Gina pulled a paperback out of her purse and read for a while. After about an hour, Shane woke up and looked over at Gina.

"Where are we?" he said.

Gina giggled and said, "When I look out of the window I see water – nothing but water everywhere."

Shane laughed and said, "I hope we aren't in the Twilight Zone." They both got a good laugh as Gina put her book away and then they talked and talked. It was a long, boring flight from Denver to Honolulu, but they both knew that it was going to be a wonderful week.

The pilot came on the speaker and told them that they would be passing by some of the other islands before touching down in Honolulu. Shane and Gina peeked out of the window and saw that there really was some land down there. Soon, they were on final approach. The touchdown was a little bumpy but they were so glad that they were now in Hawaii. The plane made its way to the terminal and soon, Shane and Gina would be stepping onto the ground in Hawaii. As they got off the plane, they were greeted in traditional Hawaiian style. A lei was placed around each of their necks and they were welcomed to Hawaii.

Shane and Gina went in the terminal and waited for their luggage. They then proceeded to the car rental counter where Bill had everything arranged for them. Getting into the car, they were now at the start of spending their first day in Hawaii. In a short time, they were arriving at their hotel on Waikiki Beach. Checking in, they got their room which was located on the eighth floor. They entered their room and immediately, Gina walked out onto the balcony. She said, "Come here, Shane, and look at this."

Shane walked onto the balcony and said, "This is so beautiful – not as beautiful as you, but beautiful."

Gina gave him a slap on the shoulder and said, "You always know the right thing to say." They turned toward each other and had their first Hawaiian kiss. It lasted for minutes and neither Shane nor Gina wanted to stop.

Shane asked if Gina wanted to change clothes and walk down to the beach. Gina said, "I have a much better idea." She pulled off Shane's shirt, and then unzipped his pants. Gina pushed him onto the bed and pulled his pants off. Pulling down his underwear and throwing them across the room, she said, "You don't need these." She turned on some slow music and stripped near the foot of the bed. Shane was excited – no other way to put it. She moved to Shane and gave him a kiss that was so passionate that Shane felt it couldn't get any better. Shane was soon to find out that it could get much better. Gina kissed every inch of Shane, rubbing her hands all over his muscular body. Shortly, Shane was on fire. He couldn't control himself any longer.

Shane grabbed ahold of Gina and flipped her over onto the bed. He kissed her lips. How he loved her lips. He wanted to kiss her forever. Shane caressed and kissed Gina everywhere. He kept kissing her and it seemed like he would never stop. Gina never wanted Shane to stop. She wanted him to enjoy her. Moving lower he circled his tongue around Gina's belly button. Gina was moaning. She was aroused. She wanted Shane. The love they were showing each other was amazing.

Both of them were sweating with passion. Shane moved up on top of her and the love making for them continued for the longest time. *What a way to start a honeymoon*, they were both thinking. He moved his lips toward hers and they kissed for the longest time. Shane rolled onto the bed and put his arms around Gina. He pulled her close and said to her, "I love you, Gina Donaldson."

Gina looked into his eyes and said, "I love you, Shane Donaldson." They both smiled and continued to stay in bed for the longest time. They fell asleep in each other's arms – not waking up until darkness had spread over the Hawaiian Islands.

It was late and Shane and Gina didn't want to get out of bed. They laid in bed hugging, kissing, talking and making love several times before the first light started to shine into their room. Shane said, "Gina, honey, the first day and night were great; however, don't you think we should get up and take a look at this beautiful island while I still have some strength left?"

Gina couldn't help but laugh as she said, "You had plenty of strength yesterday and last night, didn't you?" They both laughed and then got out of bed.

After both of them had a good shower and got cleaned up, they headed downstairs to have some breakfast. It was the start of their second day in Hawaii. Thanks to Bill, they were having the time of their lives.

Chapter Twenty-One

Shane and Gina went back to their room and changed into their swimming suits. When Shane saw Gina in her bikini, he said, "I think I'll bring the camera along."

"Ok, but I better not see any other bikinis on that camera," Gina said. They walked out onto the beach of Waikiki and looked in amazement at the beauty. It was early and many people were already out enjoying themselves. Several people greeted them as they took a stroll just taking in the beauty. Shane asked an older couple if they would mind taking a couple of photos of them.

Shane and Gina spent most of the day enjoying the sun and the water. The water was warm and Shane had always wished he was a beach bum. Gina walked toward him and gave him a hug as he came out of the water for about the tenth time. She said, "You better stay with me for a while. About every handsome young man on the beach is hitting on me. I don't know if I can keep turning them down."

Shane pulled her close and said, "Would you leave me for one of those handsome young men?"

Gina smiled and said, "Now let me think." They both laughed as they walked back together to spend some time lying in the sun.

Shane laid there and rolled over, facing Gina. He said, "Gina, are you happy?"

"Now what kind of a question is that?" she said. "I've never been happier in my life."

Shane just smiled and laid back as he said, "I saw you checking out that guy with the blonde hair that just walked by."

"Well, I saw you looking at that woman over there in the bikini with the big boobs," Gina said.

He said, "Those aren't boobs. They are built-in flotation devices. There is no way she could drown." In a minute, they were laughing hysterically.

"What do you want to do tomorrow?" Gina asked.

Shane replied, "Can we go to Pearl Harbor?" Gina thought it was a great idea but wondered why Shane wanted to go there so much. Shane told her that his grandfather was a sailor onboard the USS Arizona when the Japanese attacked Pearl Harbor on December 7, 1941. Gina saw tears welling up in Shane's eyes. She could see that it was very emotional for Shane. Shane told a little of the history of the attack on Pearl Harbor that took America into World War II.

Soon, Shane was back in the water again and Gina was wondering if he was really part fish. She looked at him – so muscular and handsome. Her life had never been better and she had been so thankful that God put both of them on the path to meeting each other. She had thanked God many times in her prayers. She wondered what life would have been like for her if it had never happened. Killing Terry – as much as she hated him – put her into a downward spiral. She felt that she was hitting rock bottom. Several times, she thought of committing suicide. Going from that feeling to the way she felt about life now was amazing.

Shane came out of the water again and came over to her. He said, "Gina Donaldson, have I told you today how much I love you?"

"Yes you have, honey, several times," she replied. He rubbed his hand over her arms and shoulders as he looked into her eyes. "Now be good big boy. We can't do it here on the beach," Gina said.

He giggled and said, "It would be fun, wouldn't it?" They were laughing so hard when Shane said, "We'd be getting sand in places that we don't want it." Now they were laughing harder than ever as they were trying to picture that in their minds.

They got up and took a stroll along the beach. Shane asked someone if they would take a photo of Shane and Gina with Diamondhead in the background. Shane thanked the woman as she said she was glad to do it. "That will look nice on the computer, won't it?" Gina said. It was a magnificent sight. They stood there looking at it for the longest time. They did some more walking along the beach, talking with people, and just enjoying each other's company. They decided to lie down on the sand again and just enjoy the view and the beautiful weather.

Shane said to Gina that it would be something living there, but it was so expensive to live in such a beautiful place. He asked Gina, "If you had a choice of anywhere to live, where would you picture yourself living?"

Gina looked at Shane and said, "I don't want to live anywhere except Change, Kansas. That was where we met. That was where God led us to."

Shane told her that she was right. Change, Kansas would be their home until their dying days. It was a special town in their hearts – like no other. Most of the day, they had been on the beach and now it was starting to get late in the afternoon.

"Are you getting hungry, my dear?" Shane asked.

"I'm getting hungry for you," Gina said.

"Will you be serious for a second? Don't you know that too much sex can kill? I barely survived last night."

Gina laughed and told Shane that he was the one asking for more last night. "I couldn't help it," Shane told her. "I was delirious!" They laughed and laughed and laughed.

Shane and Gina walked back to their hotel room and got dressed to go out for a nice dinner.

They had an enjoyable evening of dinner and dancing. "You are a good dancer," Gina said.

"That's because I used to dance with my sister," he told her.

Gina told him that he had the moves. *There must have been more than his sister in his dancing life*, she thought. Shane had his share of girlfriends growing up but only two women had ever touched his heart so deeply. Gina's life, on the other hand, had more than its fair share of sorrow. Shane knew that Gina had a tough life and he wanted to do everything in his power to make her happy.

It was late when Shane and Gina got back to their room. It had been a wonderful day – one of those days that neither one of them would ever forget. Gina came out of the bathroom and saw Shane already asleep on the bed. She smiled as she said, "Ok big boy, you get some sleep. You're going to need it in the morning." She crawled into bed and moved up close to him. She leaned over and kissed him on the cheek before saying, "I love you so much." Within minutes, she was asleep too. It had been a wonderful but exhausting day.

Chapter Twenty-Two

The third day of their honeymoon started out with them making love. Gina and Shane made love until well after breakfast time. Gina had never felt like this in her life. Even as a teenager, the guys she dated were so immature. Then, she met Terry and found out that he was a monster. God led her to Shane – the most wonderful man she had ever known. Shane loved making love and cuddling with Gina. It gave him a great feeling that he had been blessed twice in his life with wonderful wives.

It was now approaching late morning and Shane said, "Let's get a bite to eat and then we'll go to Pearl Harbor."

Gina smiled and told Shane that it was a great idea. They ate in the downstairs coffee shop. It wasn't crowded and they talked for quite a while. Gina said, "Tomorrow, can we take a drive around the island? I'd like to see as much of it as we can while we're here." Shane thought it was a great idea and both of them were looking forward to it.

They left the coffee shop and got in the car for the drive to Pearl Harbor. Looking out toward the memorial, Shane said, "There it is. My grandfather and over 900 other sailors are entombed in the sunken USS Arizona forever. Only 229 bodies were recovered."

"Oh, I didn't realize that they were permanently left on the ship," Gina said.

Shane told her that his grandfather, Pete Donaldson, was such a sweet and kind man – from what his parents had told him. He had never met Pete. Pete was only thirty-six years old when his life ended on December 7, 1941. It was an emotional time as Shane and Gina made their way to the memorial.

Shane walked to the shrine where the names of all those killed on the USS Arizona were listed. "Here is his name, Gina," Shane spoke softly. Tears were flowing down his cheeks. Gina took Shane's hand in hers. The attack on Pearl Harbor was what led the United States into World War II.

Shane was looking at the shrine when he felt someone touch his shoulder. He slowly turned around and it was Pete Donaldson. He was a ghostly image but his facial features were exactly like those seen in photos his father had shown to him. He spoke to Shane in a whisper, "Don't worry, Shane, all of my shipmates and myself are at peace." He shook Shane's hand and then looked at Gina. He said, "This must be your lovely wife. She looks very beautiful."

Shane was in awe. No one could see Pete except for Shane and Gina. Shane was crying as the ghostly image of Pete faded away. "Did you see that?" Shane asked.

"Yes, I did Shane. It was an amazing experience," Gina said. Neither one of them ever thought that they would actually see Shane's grandfather. Shane was shaking from the experience. They continued to look around and then walked out of the memorial.

Shane said, "Do you see that ship over there?" Gina just nodded her head. He said, "That is the USS Missouri. The final treaty was signed aboard that ship, ending World War II." The US war ships signaled the start and finish of America's involvement in World War II. One ship rests on the floor of the bay forever. The other ship stands guard over her sister ship. Shane couldn't help but shed many tears that day, and Gina held onto him with tears flowing down her cheeks as well. She had no idea when this day started that it would be so emotional.

Shane left that day like he had never felt in his life. It was amazing. He had seen his Grandpa Pete. Pete was standing by him. His soul was there – forever on the USS Arizona. It was a place that he would never leave and would never want to. His crewmates were with him. Pete was a hero, just like all of the others that lost their lives on that day in 1941. It had been many decades ago, but it would be a time in history that would never be forgotten. War is a terrible thing. Many people are killed, families are torn apart, and lives are never the same.

Shane and Gina got into the car and drove back to the hotel. Shane didn't say a word on the way back and Gina respected his silence. She knew what this day had meant to him. Gina could only imagine how she would feel if one of her relatives had perished in such a horrible attack. When they got back to the hotel, Shane still had tears in his eyes. He turned off the car and sat in it for a while – just staring straight ahead. Gina took ahold of his hand and said, "Are you going to be alright, honey?"

Shane turned his head toward her and said, "I'm sorry that I got so emotional. I never realized how I would feel after seeing Grandfather Pete. Did you see him, Gina? Did you see him?"

Gina smiled and said, "I know he was so happy to see you, Shane."

They both smiled and hugged each other. Shane whispered in Gina's ear, "Thank you, honey. Thank you so much."

They walked into the hotel and each got a sandwich at the coffee shop. They talked a little while they were there, but there was much silence. Gina decided it was his day and she was going to let him think about it as much as he needed to. Sometimes things happen in life where you want that special time to just take it all in without interruption. Gina sensed it. She knew that this was one of those times. They finished their sandwiches and went up to their room. Entering it, Shane walked to the balcony and sat down for a while. Gina just let him be. He stared out over the beach and the ocean wondering how a place with such beauty could also be a place of such horror. He hoped that the horror of war would never happen again.

Shane walked back into their room after about an hour. He looked at Gina and said, "Come here, beautiful." Shane held her and kissed her and didn't want to let go. She was a special woman in his heart. Shane pulled off Gina's shirt and smothered her with kisses. Soon, they were in bed sharing their love for each other. When they were done, they just laid in bed for the longest time. The thought in Gina's mind was that so many people get sex confused with love. It is possible to have sex with someone and not love them. Terry was a good example of that. With Shane, the sex and the love fit together like a puzzle. They smiled and fell asleep. It had been a long and taxing day.

Chapter Twenty-Three

Waking up early on day four of their honeymoon, Shane and Gina were both looking forward to another wonderful day. They had an early breakfast but didn't have much. Neither one of them was very hungry. They did sit at the table and had a couple of cups of coffee while they chatted. Shane was thinking to himself that Gina looked so pretty in the early morning light. After breakfast, they decided to spend a little time on the beach.

It was around ten in the morning when they decided to take a drive around the island. It was so beautiful looking at everything. Gina had noticed a large pineapple plantation on the first day of their arrival. They decided to make that their first real stop of the day. As they stepped out of the car, Gina said, "Wow, smell that Shane! Isn't it an amazing aroma?"

Shane agreed and they were both in awe as they looked out over the huge field of pineapples. They took a little tour of the pineapple plantation and they had a taste of a fresh pineapple. Shane said, "This is amazing – absolutely delicious." Gina smiled and agreed.

Continuing along, they came across several points of interest. Another was a coffee plantation. Gina said, "I didn't know they grew coffee on the island."

"I didn't either," Shane said. "We're going to have a lot to tell our friends when we get back in Kansas." He added, "Are you anxious to get back home?"

"In a way, yes, but it is amazing being here for a week," Gina replied.

Driving along, they came to an area where they saw many surfers. "Just look at the size of those waves," Shane said to Gina.

"Would you like to try it?" she asked.

Shane told her, "No, there is no way that I would do that. I much prefer dry land." Gina put her arms around Shane and asked him if he was chicken. Shame smiled and said, "I would much rather be a live chicken than a dead duck." They both laughed and gave each other a kiss.

It was when they were coming back around the loop of the island that they saw a sign that told of a Hawaiian Luau. Gina told Shane that they had to go to it. "There is no way we can be in Hawaii and not go to a Luau," Gina pleaded.

Shane agreed that it would be a wonderful thing to experience. They walked in the office and made reservations for that night. Just as darkness was overtaking Oahu, they arrived for the Luau. They walked around and met many people from all over the world. They exchanged email addresses with many of them and were hoping that it was the start of good friendships.

The food was delicious that night and Shane and Gina were both stuffed. The entertainment was fantastic. They both loved the music and dancing. As the hula dancers were performing, one of the dancers coaxed Gina up onto the stage. She didn't want to go but they wouldn't take no for an answer. Gina started out a little slow but with some teaching from the dancers, she was actually quite good. As she walked back to Shane, she felt embarrassed until he told her how good she was. He said, "Don't worry, I got some good photos. Wait until everyone sees these." They both thought that the Luau was one of the nicest things they had done on their trip.

They got back to their hotel room late that night. Both of them were so excited that they couldn't sleep. Gina kissed Shane and said, "Since we can't sleep anyway, why let this time go to waste." Shane might not have been the smartest man in the world, but it didn't take a genius to know what Gina had in mind. She unbuttoned his shirt and rubbed her hands all over Shane's chest. Gina loved feeling his muscles. She knew he was getting turned on and a wonderful night of making love was happening in their hotel room on Waikiki Beach.

Rolling over onto their backs, Gina said, "This has been the best day, sweetheart."

"Yes, it has honey. Yes it has," Shane told her.

They laid in bed and talked some more. Finally, around three in the morning, they fell asleep. Gina was snuggled up close to Shane. Shane had his arms around Gina – holding her close. They slept late that day and were amazed when they finally woke up to find that it was just a few minutes before noon. Neither one of them wanted to get out of bed. They just cuddled for the longest time. Gina said, "You know what I like about this?"

"No, what?" Shane replied.

"We can do anything we want today. It's our day. No plans – just take the day as it goes." she said.

It was well into the afternoon of day five when they finally got out of bed. They both showered. They got dressed for an afternoon on the beach and headed downstairs for some breakfast. Shane looked across the table at Gina and smiled as he thought to himself how radiant she looked that afternoon. Sipping their last cup of coffee, they strolled out of the hotel and found a nice spot on the beach. They stretched out on a blanket and let the sun warm them up. Gina liked to watch the waves. She could do it for hours. Shane liked meeting people on the beach. He had met people from all over the world on this trip. No matter where people come from, they have the same feeling inside. They all want to be happy. And looking around, Shane could see that everyone was.

Gina looked at him as he was smiling and said, "Why are you looking so happy? Are you looking at another bikini?"

He laid back down on the blanket, smiled and said, "Only yours, my dear – only yours."

Gina laid there and looked at him smiling. She was so happy to spend quality time with Shane on this trip. She knew that someday Terry would be a distant memory. Gina was thinking about how different Terry and Shane were. It was like night and day. Gina turned to Shane and asked him if he would like to live in Hawaii all the time. He told her it was nice to visit but he would be glad to get back to Change, Kansas. She asked why and he said, "Because that is where I met you, honey. I love you." Gina smiled and kissed Shane. She was so happy.

The fifth day was coming to an end. Two more to go and they would be heading home. Shane and Gina spent as much time as they could the next couple of days enjoying Oahu. The weather was beautiful, the scenery was beautiful, and the people were so pleasant.

Chapter Twenty-Four

It was time for Shane and Gina to leave Hawaii and head back to the mainland. They drove the car to the airport and Shane turned in the rental car. They checked in and waited for their flight. Both of them seemed kind of quiet. It had been a glorious week – thanks to Bill. They sat in the terminal and talked about how kind Joe and Bill had been to them. Gina said, "We have to do something when we get back home to thank them for their kindness." Shane nodded his head and agreed. They were two amazing people and Shane and Gina were thankful to have them in their lives.

It was time to board the plane and when it took off, Gina could see tears in Shane's eyes. She didn't say anything. She just watched him. As the plane lifted off and flew over Pearl Harbor, she heard him say, "Goodbye, Grandpa Pete." He then turned his head away from Gina because he didn't want her to see him crying.

Gina reached over and took Shane's hand in hers and said, "I understand, honey. I really do." Lifting up into the clear blue sky, they were now heading home after the trip of their lives.

It would be a long time before they would land in Denver. Gina took a paperback out of her purse and read for the longest time. Shane glanced through a magazine and then took a nap. It was fun being in Hawaii but it was also tiring. Gina glanced over at him and smiled saying, "I guess the love making wore you out. You are going to be tired for years to come." Gina got tired of reading and put the paperback back in her purse. She rested her head on Shane's shoulder and fell asleep. She didn't want to admit it, but she was very tired.

Shane woke up first and noticed Gina sleeping on his shoulder. It made him smile as he leaned over and kissed her on the cheek. Gina moved a little and then was dead still. Shane was thinking about the trip and how it was so relaxing and so much fun. He couldn't wait to get back home and thank everyone and tell them how much they meant to him and Gina. They would have to write out some thank you cards to send to everyone who came to the wedding. It had only been a week since the wedding, but it seemed like it had been longer. The pilot came on the loud speaker and said they would be in Denver in about an hour. It would be a couple of hours on the ground and then the final leg of their flight from Denver to Wichita.

They would be glad to get back home and back to work. Shane was sure that at this time of the year, Bill would be overloaded with work. That was good. Shane thought he might be able to pick up some overtime. The extra money would come in handy now. Gina had always made good tips at the diner. It was in their minds to save as much money as they could. They had quite a bit saved but they wanted more to put toward a down payment for their own home. Shane had been looking at some houses in Change. The prices were very reasonable and he was sure that in the not too distant future, they would be home owners.

The plane touched down in Denver and Shane and Gina sat in the airport terminal talking for the longest time. They did get a little bite to eat in the cafeteria before they boarded the next flight to Wichita. Gina said, "I'm getting anxious to get back home and see everyone."

"So am I," Shane replied. It was a little bit of a bumpy ride because of thunderstorms between Denver and Wichita.

As the plane was on final approach to the Wichita airport, Shane and Gina held hands. They were almost there and as the wheels touched the runway, Gina said, "We're finally home."

Shane replied, "Yes, we are. It was a wonderful trip but I'm glad we're back."

Shane and Gina arrived at the baggage claim area and were met by a crowd of about twenty-five people. Standing in the front were Joe and Bill holding up signs saying, "WELCOME HOME!!!!" Everyone had signs and balloons and were cheering. Shane and Gina never expected this. Gina ran to Joe and gave him a big hug with tears in her eyes. Shane shook Bill's hand and hugged him and thanked him for the trip. Then, everyone gathered around and hugged and kissed Shane and Gina. The cheering calmed down for a minute and Shane said, "Thank you everyone. We never expected to be greeted by such wonderful friends. The honeymoon was great but we are glad to be home in Change, Kansas." The cheering started again. Shane and Gina got their luggage and were followed out of the airport. Bill gave them a ride back to their apartment.

Arriving back at their apartment, they were so glad to get home. Shane and Gina thanked Bill for the ride from the airport. They went inside and left their suitcases in the living room. Shane looked into his bedroom and said, "No more separate bedrooms, sweetie. You can sleep in here now."

Gina looked in and pushed Shane on the bed. She said, "Before I can sleep in here, I have to check out the mattress." As tired as they were, they were making love in a matter of minutes.

"Are you ever too tired?"

Gina said laughingly, "No honey, never."

The trip was long and after making love, they wanted to sleep forever. They laid on the bed naked – in each other's arms as their eyes closed. After sleeping for over twelve hours straight, they just laid there awake for the longest time – not wanting to move. Gina said, "Do you want to get up?"

Shane replied, "No. After I get some more sleep." They both laughed and closed their eyes again.

Chapter Twenty-Five

As Shane and Gina woke up the next day, they realized that they were back in the real world, and it was time to go back to work. Gina walked in the diner with a smile on her face. All of the other waitresses welcomed her back. One of them yelled for Joe. He came out and gave Gina a big hug and welcomed her back. How was the honeymoon, everyone wanted to know? Gina told them that it was fabulous – the trip of a lifetime. She gave them a little story of what it was like and then customers started to come into the diner for breakfast. It was time to start earning a living again.

Shane showed up at his work. Bill was equally glad to see him back. Bill knew that Shane would help him get caught up with his work again. Bill said, "Would you like to work some overtime?" Shane was glad to get it and Bill was glad he was eager to do it. Bill asked him how the honeymoon was. Shane said they had the time of their lives. Bill said with a grin, "How long did it take you to get out of the hotel room?"

Shane's face turned a little red and he replied, "It was sometime during the second day." Bill was happy for Shane. He thought Gina was such a beautiful woman.

Shane stopped at the diner on the way home to meet Gina. When he walked in, everyone surrounded him and wanted to know more about the honeymoon. Shane's face turned red again and said, "Are you girls trying to get me to tell you things that are secret between Gina and I?"

They all said, "Yes, come on, tell us more." They all laughed and pointed at Shane's red face.

"Gina, are you going to help me?" Shane said. "I'm under attack." Everyone was laughing – even Gina.

Gina grabbed onto his arm and said, "Let's get out of here." They walked out the door and headed home hand in hand.

"They make a really nice couple, don't they?" said Joe. Everyone agreed that they really did.

They got home and talked about their first day back at work. Shane said, "Bill wants me to work some overtime until he gets caught up." They agreed that it was good because they could save some money to get a down payment for a house. It was their dream to have their own house. They both could picture just what they wanted. A cute house with a nice yard and a white picket fence in the front was what they both wanted.

"We need a nice yard in a quiet neighborhood so the kids have a good place to play," Gina said. Shane looked at Gina thinking that having children was something they had never talked about. Shane loved kids and smiled at Gina as he pictured in his head the children running around in the yard.

They were going to have to save as much money as they could in the months to come. Shane was working overtime for Bill and even picked up a part-time job stocking shelves late at night in the local grocery store. Gina was working at the diner and making crafts at home that she would sell at the local flea market on weekends. Shane and Gina were both getting tired, but the money was going in the bank and they were getting closer to their dream home. Shane and Gina had both been going on the Internet to search for a home that fit what they were wanting to purchase.

It had now been almost a year since they had been back from their honeymoon. With both of them working so much, they were getting tired – very tired. Gina said one evening, "We are getting a lot of money in the bank. We have enough for a down payment, but I think we need to push ourselves a little more to get some money in the bank to fall back on." Shane agreed and looked forward to the day when they could slack off on their work a little and spend more time together. Shane and Gina were so much in love. In the year they had been married, their love had grown more and more each day.

Neither one of them left the house without kissing and saying to the other one, "I love you."

It was another six months of pushing themselves when Gina said, "We have enough money now, Shane."

Shane smiled and pulled Gina close to him. He kissed her and said, "I love you, Gina Donaldson."

Gina smiled at him with tears in her eyes and said, "I love you. I never knew anyone as nice as you existed." They were holding each other knowing that when God put them together, it was a lifetime commitment. Gina said, "Let's go to bed."

"Yes. Let's go to bed. I'm so tired," replied Shane. Gina looked at him with a smile on her face. Shane came back to reality and chuckled. He knew that Gina wasn't thinking about going to sleep right away. Shane and Gina made love every time like it was their first.

"Gina, I think one of these days you are going to kill me," Shane said.

Gina laughed and said, "You love every minute of it. You know you do." Shane couldn't disagree with that. It was incredible every time.

Shane and Gina contacted a realtor in town. They told the agent, Patty, just what they were looking for. They weren't looking for a huge house. A nice yard was something that they had to have. The white picket fence was something that they could add after they bought a house. Patty wanted to know if they wanted something right in town or a little out of town. It was something that they hadn't really thought about. They told Patty a little out of town would be nice, but they would consider something in town if it was in a quiet neighborhood. Patty said, "Give me a couple of days and I'll show you some places that I think you might like."

Patty called them in a couple of days and set up a time to view some houses. It was the fourth house that Patty showed them that they fell in love with immediately. It was right on the edge of town – a beautiful ranch-style home with three bedrooms and two baths on three-quarters of an acre of land. The front and back yards were so flat and beautiful with some nice shade trees. They couldn't believe it when they saw a fabulous white picket fence surrounding the front yard. This was what they wanted. They told Patty to get the ball rolling.

It wasn't long before everything was taken care of. Shane and Gina were now home owners. Bill and Shane did most of the moving using one of Bill's trucks. Even when moving out of an apartment, there is still a lot of heavy lifting. They started early in the morning and finished up early in the evening. Shane and Gina were so thankful for Bill's help that they took him out to dinner. Bill wished them good luck in their new home. Shane and Gina Donaldson were continuing a life of happiness.

Chapter Twenty-Six

Shane and Gina were so happy in their new home. Gina
spent a lot of time planting flowers and with the advice of
Bill, she was turning the home into a show place that anyone
would love to see. Shane was working some overtime for
Bill and he also worked a little part time. They didn't need
the money badly, but it was nice to have a little saved in the
bank in case something would happen in their lives.

It was about six months after they moved into their home
that Joe had a massive heart attack. It affected everyone at
the diner but to Gina, it was like she lost a father. Joe had
been so good to her and she talked to Shane often about the
reception he threw for them. His kindness was something
that the two of them would never forget. Gina said, "I
wonder if Joe's wife will close the diner?" Shane had never
met Joe's wife, but Gina had met her a few times. Betty
Carson was just like Joe. She cared for everyone and was
always so thoughtful. Gina called up Betty and told her how
sorry she was. Gina and Betty talked for the longest time.
Betty told Gina that Joe looked at her like she was his
daughter.

Gina said, "I know when Sara died it was very tough on
Joe. He told me of the story of her cancer with tears in his
eyes."

"Yes, Joe took it very hard. He loved Sara so much,"
Betty said. She wanted to know if Gina and Shane would be
at the viewing and the funeral. Betty gave Gina the times

and Gina told her they would be there. Gina and Shane walked into the funeral home the night of the viewing. All of the waitresses from the diner were there. Every one of them looked at Joe in the coffin with tears in her eyes. Gina was particularly upset and the tears just flowed and flowed. Gina hugged Betty and told her that Joe was a wonderful, sweet, and kind man. They stayed in the funeral home until everyone was leaving. Gina wanted to do everything she could to comfort Betty.

Betty walked up to Shane and said, "Shane, I need one more pallbearer at tomorrow's funeral."

"Betty, it would be my honor."

She smiled at him and gave him a big hug. "Thank you, thank you so much," she replied.

Gina smiled at Shane and said, "Thank you for doing that. I know it means a lot to Betty." Shane agreed that it was a tough time for her right now. Joe went so quickly and Shane wondered how it would affect Gina if he went to work one day and never returned home. It is an awful thing to think about, but it was a reality of life that could happen.

Gina and Shane talked about it on the way home and Gina said, "Promise me one thing, Shane. Promise me you will never leave the house without hugging and kissing me."

Shane smiled before saying, "That is one promise that will be very easy for me to keep."

The next day as they entered the church, everyone was in a quiet state of mind. Joe had so many friends in town. Everyone had been in his diner at one time or another. Joe was a great community man and loved helping others. Betty saw Gina and Shane come in and asked Gina to please sit with her. Gina was glad to do it. Hundreds of people filled the church. It was an amazing display of love. Betty leaned over to Gina and said, "Will you come over to the house after we leave the cemetery? I don't want to be alone for a little while." Gina told her that they would be glad to.

It was nearing the end of the church service when the reverend pulled a piece of paper out of his pocket that Betty had given to him. Joe didn't plan on having a heart attack but he gave this paper to Betty years ago and told her that if anything ever happened to him that he wanted it read at his funeral. The reverend looked at the paper and read it silently. He then said, "Betty gave me this piece of paper and asked me to read it. It was written by Joe some years ago." The reverend looked at Betty. She smiled and then he smiled before he proceeded: "You are all my friends here. I want you to remember me with a smile on your face and a warm feeling in your heart. Don't remember me with sadness or tears. I don't want to be remembered that way. I love you all." It was such a touching moment.

Shane and the other pallbearers carried the coffin to the waiting hearse. It was soon on its way to the cemetery. About fifty people showed up there and gave their final prayers for Joe. No one was ever going to forget him. Most people saw Joe as the kindest man in Change, Kansas. It was a tough day for everyone, but especially tough for Betty and Gina. Except for Shane, Joe was the man that she cared more about than anyone. As soon as she started working at the diner, Joe took Gina under his wing.

With the day coming to a close, Gina and Shane went with Betty to her home. It was a beautiful house and they found out from Betty that Joe did much of the building of it himself. Shane wondered how he could have done that and kept up working such long hours at the diner. Betty said, "The diner was Joe's life. He gave away so many free meals to people that were down on their luck. I really loved that man." Kindness is what Joe was all about. Betty said, "Gina, I need you to do me a favor."

"Sure, Betty – anything," Gina replied.

Betty sat silent for a few minutes and then said, "I want you to call up everyone that works at the diner and tell them we will be opening for breakfast the day after tomorrow. Will you do that for me?" Gina smiled and told her she surely would. Everyone there was wondering if the diner was going to stay closed so it would be a relief to them to know they still had a job.

Shane and Gina left Betty's and went to their own home. Gina made call after call and told everyone of the news. Gina told all of the employees that Betty had told her that if anything ever happened to Joe that he wanted the diner to stay open. Gina hung up the phone after the last call, looked up and said, "Thank you for everything, Joe. I love you." She knew that he was looking down on her knowing that everything was going to be alright.

Chapter Twenty-Seven

On the morning of the diner reopening, all of the employees were there. Mingling around, they all talked about how wonderful Joe was and what a tragedy it was that his life was cut too short. The doors were still locked and Betty showed up and thanked everyone for being there. Betty and all of the employees walked inside and Betty locked the door behind her. She asked everyone to sit in the corner of the diner as she got ready to say a few words.

Betty told everyone that she loved them all. "Joe would often come home from work and tell me stories of all of you," she said. She expressed how Joe felt about each and every one of them. He never looked at any of them as employees. He looked at them as family. Betty wanted to know if everyone was going to stay on working at the diner. It was unanimous. Everyone loved Joe and they wanted to stay.

Tammy, one of the waitresses that worked longer than anyone else, asked Betty if she could say something. She had something in her hands that was covered up. She said, "After I left the funeral the other day, I went home and cried. Then, I realized that Joe didn't want us to do that. I had to do something in his honor, so I did this painting of Joe." When she uncovered the painting, everyone thought it was the nicest tribute to Joe. Betty gave Tammy a big hug and thanked her for doing such a thoughtful thing.

"What do you all say we hang this on the wall dead center in the diner so it is seen by everyone when they walk through the door?" said Betty.

"That is a wonderful idea. It is a great tribute to Joe," Gina replied.

Betty talked for a little while and knew that someone was going to have to be in charge. She made Tammy in charge of the wait staff. Chris, who had been Joe's cook for years, was in charge of the kitchen. Betty said, "I'll be the overall manager of the diner, but I need help in knowing when food and supplies need to be ordered." Chris and Tammy were more than glad to do their part. Betty said, "I know Joe is looking down on us right now and he is smiling at seeing how everyone is coming together to keep his diner thriving."

Gina wanted to know how long Joe had the diner. Betty told her that it was just shy of twenty-three years. Everyone smiled and expressed their love for Joe.

"I have an idea, Betty, and I want to know how you feel about it. What if we changed the name of the diner from Diner of Change to Joe's Diner?" Gina asked.

Betty thought about it for a few minutes with tears in her eyes. Betty wanted to know what everyone else thought of the idea. All of the employees thought the idea was fabulous. Betty said, "We'll have a new sign on the building soon. Thanks, all of you, for your kindness toward Joe." Everyone got up and hugged Betty and told her how thankful they were that she decided to keep the diner open. She said, "Everyone, Joe and I talked about this often and decided if anything happened to him, I would do everything in my power to keep the diner open."

The diner opened a little late for breakfast that morning and all of Joe's regulars were lined up at the door. Betty unlocked the door and let them in. All of the customers hugged Betty and it was so emotional for her. Gina took

Betty aside and asked her how she was going to cope financially. Betty smiled at Gina and thanked her for being concerned. Betty said, "Don't worry about me, Gina. Joe had taken out an insurance policy that will keep me living comfortably for the rest of my life."

Everything was running fine and Betty knew that Joe had employees that loved him. Betty kept the books herself and she could see in no time at all that the diner was still thriving. It was two weeks later when the sign company took down the old sign and raised the sign officially making it, Joe's Diner. It was an honor for Betty to see her husband's name on the building where he had spent twenty-three years of his life serving the finest food to the people of Change, Kansas. Gina stayed a little late that night cleaning up in the dining area and Betty was in the office doing the books. Gina walked in and said, "Betty, would you like to have a cup of coffee?"

"I'm done in here, Gina, but yes, I would like to have some coffee. What do you say we go sit at a booth and have some pie to go along with that coffee?" Gina just smiled and got the pie and coffee and took it to a booth.

Gina could see that Betty was tired. "It's been tough on you, hasn't it?" Gina said.

Betty told her she was tired but having all of the people here at the diner being so kind made it a lot easier. Gina told Betty that she would never forget Joe. "Joe really loved you, Gina. It was tough on him when Sara died, but when you came into his life, it was like he was a new man," Betty assured her.

"I was so glad Joe gave me away at the wedding." Gina said. "You have no idea how much it meant to me."

"You have no idea how much it meant to Joe. He talked about it for days," Betty said.

Shane showed up at the door and tapped on it. Betty let him in and said, "Gina and I have just been talking. Would you like some pie and coffee?"

"That would be nice, thanks," he said.

They all said it had been a long day and the pie and coffee really hit the spot. Shane asked Betty how she was holding up. She told him that it was good for her to come into the diner. She missed Joe so much, and not seeing Joe come home from work every day was tough.

Shane told Betty how sorry he was and then added, "The new sign and the portrait will keep Joe's memory alive forever." She told Shane how pleased she was that Tammy had done the portrait.

As they all left the diner that night, they said to each other, "Have a good night."

Shane turned around and saw Betty walking away. He stopped in his tracks for a few minutes and thought how old she looked. Gina said, "She'll be alright, Shane. She has a lot of good friends. When the shock of Joe's death eases, I'm sure she will be alright." Shane nodded his head yes and the two of them walked to their home.

Chapter Twenty-Eight

The diner was thriving more than it ever had. Betty knew that if Joe was looking down on it, he would be so proud of his wife and all of the employees. Shane and Gina were home one night and Gina said, "Do you think Betty will keep the diner forever or will she sell it?"

"I've thought about that very thing myself," Shane replied. "The diner is doing great, but Betty really doesn't need the money. I think more than anything, she is keeping it open in Joe's honor." They talked about it a little more and both felt that in time, she would sell it.

So many things were going through Shane's and Gina's minds that night. Shane said, "Gina, have you ever seen a person in Change, Kansas who was nasty or mean? Have you ever seen anyone here ever get into trouble? Have you ever seen anyone commit a crime? This must be the only little city in America that doesn't have a police force."

Gina thought about what Shane was saying. It did seem strange to her. There was no doubt in her mind that they weren't the only people that God had sent to the city of Change. Gina said, "It is a beautiful city – the most beautiful I have ever been in. It is something that I have never seen one piece of litter anywhere in the city."

Shane and Gina talked about it for hours. They wondered how old the city was. There was a mayor and some other elected local officials; however, as Shane had brought up, there was no police force. No doubt, there was no need for it. God had picked certain people to send here – people that He knew could show nothing but love. It was His way of making a little piece of heaven in America.

Bill and Shane were doing a lot of landscaping. It impressed Shane because every place in town was kept looking so beautiful. Shane said to Bill, "How long have you lived here?"

"I've been here a little over twenty years," Bill replied. "I was passing through town one day and met Jeannie. We've been married twenty years now. You've met our two boys. They are great kids."

Shane told Bill that he had a wonderful family. Bill told him thanks. They meant the world to him. Bill did say, "Isn't this a wonderful place to live? Everyone is so kind and sweet here."

Shane went home that night and told Gina what Bill had told him. Gina said, "I talked with some of the other wait-resses and got very similar stories. All of them had come to Change and had met their husbands here." Shane and Gina both loved it here and they had so many friends. They both had their journeys arranged by God. There was no doubt now that everyone else in town had been sent there by God.

"I want to talk with Reverend Tillman," Shane said. "If anyone has a story to tell about how this city started, he would know."

Gina agreed that it might be a good idea to talk to him. "Life goes on here. Babies are born and people grow old and die. However, there is something different about here," noted Gina.

The next day when Shane was driving home, he saw the reverend just entering the steps to the church. Shane decided it was a good time to have a talk. Shane walked inside the church and said to Reverend Tillman, "If you aren't too busy, could we have a talk?"

"Sure, Shane, I always have time to talk to you."

Shane told the reverend that he had many wonders about how the city got started. He told the reverend it was a wonderful city, however, it seemed to him that God had picked certain people to meet here.

Reverend Tillman smiled at Shane before he said, "You are right, Shane. God only picks certain people to spend their lives here. He sees kindness and love in people."

"Do you talk to God? Does He come here?" Shane asked.

Reverend Tillman spoke in a low voice, "Yes, Shane, God does appear before me on occasion. He wants to know how everyone is doing. He loves all of you very much."

Continuing, the reverend told Shane stories of how people ended up there. Almost all of them had tragedies in their lives. They then had depression, but God saw the good side of them. He knows that Gina killed her husband; however, Gina went through years of abuse, both physically and emotionally. Gina is a wonderful woman filled with kindness. The reverend then said, "No one is a prisoner here, Shane. Anyone can leave at any time. Do you notice that no one wants to leave? This city is filled with love and kindness."

Shane was nodding his head and admitted that there was a lot of love in this city. Reverend Tillman asked, "Do you and Gina like it here in Change?"

"Oh yes, we love it here and never want to leave. We were just wondering about how the city came to be," Shane replied.

Shane stood up and thanked Reverend Tillman for talking with him. Reverend Tillman shook Shane's hand and thanked him for coming in.

Shane left the church feeling so at peace. He went home and talked with Gina for hours about what the reverend had said. Gina said, "We were lucky, Shane. We are part of a chosen few. As you can see, this is a small city. There is nothing here but love."

Shane had just one major question which the reverend did answer. He wanted to know: if this is a little piece of heaven on earth, then why do people have to die? Reverend Tillman had told him that was life. People are born and people die. That would never change.

Shane and Gina went to bed that night feeling so at peace. In bed, they talked until after midnight before falling asleep. Shane woke up early and walked into the kitchen to put the coffee on to brew. He sat at the table and had one cup – just thinking to himself. It could have been anyone that God chose to spend his life with Gina. It was him and he would be forever thankful that such a sweet, kind, and beautiful woman came into his life. Sure, there were still times when he thought of Becky. She was his first love and their life together ended tragically. Shane now realized that he could love again. Gina was standing in the doorway to the kitchen and said, "You look like you are in deep thought. Is there anything wrong?"

Standing up, Shane walked to Gina, put his arms around her and kissed her like it was the first time. Gina said, "Well, I'm pretty sure now that there is nothing wrong." They hugged and smiled at each other.

They had a good breakfast before heading off to their jobs. They were happy – very happy – and that meant so much to both of them. They both walked into work with smiles on their faces. Everyone wanted to know what was on their minds. They both said there was nothing. They were just so happy to have such nice friends.

Chapter Twenty-Nine

The regulars were coming into Joe's Diner that morning and sitting at their regular booths or tables. Everyone was so happy and that was because all of the waitresses made them feel at home. When there was a little slack time, they always liked to talk with their customers. Many of them seemed like family, but that is the way it was supposed to be.

There was a supply salesman who came into the diner and had a long talk with Betty. Betty took an instant liking to him and all of the waitresses were buzzing around that it looked like more than business. It had been more than a year since Joe died. Betty was lonesome at times, even though she had such good friends. Joe and Betty had talked for years that if either one of them died, the other should remarry if they found the right person. This salesman had only come into the diner this one time but everyone felt that there would be a lot more visits.

He came into the diner about every other week. Everyone knew that it wasn't just a business call. He was a quiet man and appeared a little bit shy. Gina asked him one day where he was from. He said, "Originally, I'm from back east but for some reason I seem drawn here. It's like a magnet is pulling me."

Gina wanted to know if he was married and he said, "No, my wife died about four years ago."

Gina told him how tough it is when a loved one dies. She said, "Betty lost her husband a little over a year ago." He told Gina that Betty was a really nice woman.

Love comes in strange ways, Gina thought. She thought back to when Shane and Gina had met in the park. Both of them had walked well over a thousand miles on journeys that were arranged by God. Gina knew that it was worth every step of the way. God knew they needed time to think. They needed to meet people and find out just how nice people can be. Gina would be the first to admit that Terry still haunted her sometimes. You can't be abused for years and then just forget about it. Gina knew that to look at her, no one would think she could shoot and kill anyone. As she looked around Change, Kansas, she could see nothing but love; however, she knew also that there were a lot of bad people in the world. She was thinking that things would work out for Betty, hoping that the new man in her life would bring her happiness the way Joe did.

It took a long time but the salesman decided to move to Change. The salesman, Jim Jenkins, and Betty became inseparable and everyone knew that there would be a wedding on the horizon. It was one morning a few months later when the two of them walked into the diner with an announcement. The announcement was that Jim had proposed to Betty and she said yes. Everyone cheered and hugged both of them. Love was in everyone. Love is what it is all about. Soon, Reverend Tillman would be performing another ceremony. He had married many couples in Change and he knew that there would be many more to follow.

It was a few months later when Betty and Jim were married in the little church. Shane, Gina, Betty, and Jim would become good friends. Betty didn't want Jim to be a salesman any longer. It would often take him away from home. She worried about him when he was gone. It was after one of his trips when she asked him if he would like to learn the business at the diner. Jim was a hardworking man and Betty knew he would fit right in with everyone there. Betty announced to all of the employees that Jim would be joining them in the business. He would eventually be doing what Joe did there. It took him some time to learn how to cook in a diner, how to meet and greet people, and how to keep the books. Betty was thinking that she wouldn't have to work as much.

Shane and Gina sat at home one night having a cup of coffee and talking about their days at work. Shane wanted to know how it was working out with Jim. Gina said, "He is a nice man – so pleasant and thoughtful. I think Betty married him because he reminds people so much of Joe."

"Yes, he is nice but no one will ever forget Joe," Shane said.

"Joe was like a father to me. I'll never forget everything he did for us," replied Gina. Shane poured another cup of coffee for Gina and himself. They talked for the longest time about how much they loved it there.

Life in Change, Kansas was good. It was very, very good. When Gina first met Shane on that park bench a long time ago, she had no idea that life could be as good as it now was. She thought of how she was so afraid of Terry and how much she loved Shane. Shane was a remarkable man. His kindness and consideration was something that made Gina smile every day. *Nothing is more wonderful than spending your life with the man you love*, she thought. Every day she got compliments, hugs, and kisses and often wished the day would never end. Shane had the same feeling. He still thought about Becky, but not as much as he used too.

Shane came home the next day and said, "Let's take a vacation. Where would you like to go?"

"I don't know. Let me think about it," Gina said. It was a few days later when Shane met her at the diner after work. They sat at a booth and Gina told Shane where she wanted to go. "I've never been there, Shane, but I've been told the New England states are so beautiful in the autumn," Gina said.

Shane smiled and said he had never been there either. It was getting to be late summer and in a few months, the leaves would be turning color in New England. They went online later that night and found a beautiful country inn in Vermont. They made reservations for early October – when the leaves were expected to be the most beautiful.

Gina told Betty she wanted that week off and naturally, Betty approved it with no problem. Shane gave his notice to Bill and he also wished them great weather and a beautiful fun-filled time. Bill had actually grown up in New England and gave Shane a list of some places they might like to visit. Shane went home that night and pulled Bill's list up on the computer. There were so many interesting things to see. They knew they were going to have a wonderful time.

They would fly to Boston and then get on a little puddle jumper to fly into central Vermont. There, they would rent a car and take the hour drive to the country inn. They were counting the days until it was vacation time. Betty and Bill were going to miss them, but they knew that everyone had to get away from work every now and then to get in some relaxation time.

Chapter Thirty

Early October had finally come around and Shane and Gina were on their way for a vacation in New England. They picked a beautiful old country inn in central Vermont. They loved Change, Kansas but no matter where people live, they need to get away once in a while. Change was a laid-back city. There was no hustle and bustle of everyday life as seen in many areas of the country. Shane and Gina were sitting in the airport in Boston waiting for their connecting flight that would take them to Vermont.

"Look at how people are rushing around like it is a matter of life and death," Shane said to Gina.

"I know. No one is smiling," Gina replied. "I hope their faces don't freeze that way."

They both laughed. It seemed so funny to them. Shane said, "You know, Gina, I was just like that before I went on my journey to Change. Even on the walk, my outlook on life changed. I looked at things differently. Then, when I walked into that city, I knew that my life was changing forever."

"It was a little different for me. I was held like a prisoner," Gina said. "Terry had me constantly in fear for my life. I didn't have much contact with the outside world. My walk started to change me. I became more trusting of people. When I walked into that city park and met you, I knew and could feel that my life was going to be better. I love you, Shane, very much."

Shane smiled and held Gina's hand. Just then, it was announced that it was time to board the little plane that would take them to Vermont. Gina looked out of the plane's window and could see the bright colors of the leaves. She told Shane to look and they stared in amazement. When they landed, they could feel a chill in the autumn air. Gina said, "I'm glad we packed some sweaters and jackets."

They proceeded to get their luggage and then to the rental counter to get their car. Getting into the car, Shane said, "We'll be there soon."

Gina told him that she couldn't wait to get settled. It was about an hour later when they pulled into a beautiful, old, rustic country inn. The sign said, "WELCOME TO SCENIC VIEW." They got out of their car and just looked off into the distance. The view was fantastic and the colors of the leaves made them realize they had made a wise decision on coming here.

They went inside and were welcomed by a couple about ten years older than themselves. They owned the inn. Shane said, "Hi, we're the Donaldson's."

Paul shook hands with both of them and said, "Welcome, so nice to meet you. This is my wife Peggy."

Peggy gave them a sweet welcome, as Shane and Gina checked in. Gina said, "We heard it is so beautiful in Vermont this time of the year."

"When the leaves turn color, it's often said that it is God's country," Peggy said. They got their key and walked upstairs to a lovely room with a private bath. It had that New England charm of days gone by.

"This is gorgeous," Gina said.

They got dressed a little warmer and walked downstairs. They sat down for a while and chatted with Paul and Peggy. Paul and Peggy came from Atlanta about twenty years ago and fell in love with the place. They bought it a few years later and loved owning and operating the inn.

Peggy came up with the name for the sign because of the beautiful view. Shane said, "It is an amazing view." Paul told them that as they drove around, they would see many spectacular views. Paul even told them of a few roads to take where they would see some of the area's most beautiful sights.

Gina said, "As we were driving in, we passed an old country store. It looked like a place I would like to visit."

"Oh, you must go there. They have so many things that you don't see anywhere else. You won't see anything in China made there. Everything is made in America and much is made by local craftsmen," Peggy said.

Shane and Gina thought that was fabulous. Paul and Peggy told them of other places around that would take them back in time. Paul said, "It's like you stepped back a hundred years."

"Breakfast is served from 7 to 9 a.m. Lunch will be up to you," Peggy said. "I can suggest a nice local diner that has the best food. We serve dinner from 6 to 8 p.m. If you like, you can give me your order earlier in the day. Tell us what time and I'll have it ready for you then."

"That is awesome. I really think we're going to like it here," Shane said.

Shane and Gina told them they were going to take a little drive and take some photos.

Driving around, they found that the bright-colored leaves were so beautiful. It was cool, so they both wore a light jacket. Gina said, "I bet it gets cold here at night."

Shane replied, "Don't worry, baby. I have a sure way to warm up."

She laughed and said, "I bet you do." They saw a few small lakes in the area and stopped at one of them. Shane told Gina that he would like to do a little fishing.

"Me too. It will be fun," Gina said.

Shane had brought along the tripod. He set the camera timer and took some photos of him and Gina with the lake in the background. He was wondering if there were any hiking trails close by. Gina said, "We'll ask Paul and Peggy when we get back."

They didn't stay out long the first day. Both of them were kind of tired from the long trip. Paul and Peggy were both sitting in rocking chairs on the front porch when they arrived. Shane asked about hiking trails and if they could fish anywhere nearby. Paul drew a little map for them and showed where there were some great hiking trails. Paul said, "Several of these trails have lakes on them that you can fish at. You can get a license at that little store you were talking about earlier."

"If you catch a couple fish and want to have them for dinner, I can do that for you," Peggy said.

Shane and Gina told them how kind they were. Shane said, "You have a nice place here. I'm glad we picked your place to stay at."

"We're so glad to have you," Peggy said. "We hope you enjoy your stay and will come back again."

They all sat on the front porch and talked for a couple of hours. Shane and Gina learned that winters could be rough, but the scenery was so beautiful when the snow was falling. Peggy got up and said, "I have to get dinner started for the other guests. If you would like something quick, I can make it for you."

"No thanks, we're more tired than hungry. We'll let you know tomorrow morning what we'd like to have for tomorrow's dinner," Gina said.

Paul stayed and talked to them a while longer. Gina said, "I guess we'll go up to our room and get a good night's sleep. We'll see you at breakfast, Paul."

"Goodnight, folks. Sleep well." Then, he went in to give Peggy a hand with dinner.

The next morning, Shane and Gina went down for breakfast at 7:30 a.m. It was a fabulous breakfast and Peggy went all out to please her guests. When they finished, Shane and Gina went outside and took a nice walk in the brisk morning air. It was still very cool, but it looked like another bright sunny day was coming up for them. They just hung around the inn until about 10:30 when they decided to go to the country store. Gina was in awe as she walked in. She couldn't get over all of the crafts. Shane had a feeling he wasn't going to be able to get out of there for several hours. Shane and Gina also picked up their fishing licenses and a couple of cheap fishing poles. The man behind the counter said, "You can purchase bait here."

"Great, maybe tomorrow," said Shane. "Today, we're going to take a hike."

Shane drove to a spot that Paul had told him about. It was a nice trail leading up a nearby mountain. A few spots along the trail, the views were incredible. Naturally, Gina wanted to take some photos. It was now early afternoon and the air was warming up nicely. They brought a couple of sandwiches with them and some bottled water. There was a large rock about twenty yards from the trail. Shane said, "Let's go over behind that rock and have our lunch."

"Ok, it sounds great," Gina said. They walked back there and found a flat, little grassy area where they ate their sandwiches. Shane and Gina were thinking about so many things. Suddenly, Shane jumped up and started to gather leaves and laid them down on the grassy area.

Wondering what he was doing, Gina just stared at him for the longest time. Finally, she had to say, "What are you doing?"

He stayed silent and finally had leaves a few inches thick. He moved his hands over the leaves and pressed down on them. Holding out his hand, he pulled Gina up. He said, "Well, what do you think?"

"What do I think about what?"

Shane smiled at her. He unbuttoned her shirt, removed her bra, and then kissed her breasts. Within minutes, Shane and Gina were making love on the pile of leaves. Gina said, "That was incredible! I never did it like that. That was good. No, it was better than good."

Shane pulled her close and they laid still and kissed on the pile of leaves. Gina said, "What if someone comes and sees us?"

Shane laughed and said, "They will see two people – naked and in love – lying on a pile of leaves."

Gina leaned over and kissed Shane before saying, "I love you."

Shane said, "Years ago, we walked to love. Today, it was a shorter walk, but we walked to love again."

"Do you know you are a crazy man, Shane Donaldson?" Gina said.

Shane thought for a minute and said, "Yes, I admit I'm crazy – in love with you." They got dressed and walked back to the car. Arriving back at the Scenic View Inn, they saw Paul sitting out on the front porch.

Paul just had to ask, "Hi, folks. Did you do anything exciting today?" Shane's face turned red as a beet and Gina turned away and giggled.

"Paul, have you ever made love in a pile of leaves?" she said.

They could see Paul was embarrassed but he said, "No, I can't say that I've ever done that." The rest of the time during their stay, Paul never asked again if they had an exciting day.

The next day, they went fishing and caught a couple of nice trout. Peggy fixed them up and served them to Shane and Gina for dinner. They were delicious. Every meal that Peggy made for them during their stay was wonderful. The rest of the time they stayed at the inn, they took long walks or drove around the countryside. They loved their stay there and thought that maybe they would return. They thought that the nicest part of their vacation – other than making love on the pile of leaves – was sitting on the front porch every day chatting with Paul and Peggy. One day when Peggy and Gina were sitting on the porch alone, Peggy got the biggest smile on her face. "Gina, Paul told me what you said the other day. I laughed and I laughed. I wish I had been out here to hear you say that."

"I didn't mean to embarrass Paul but it was good," said Gina. "I mean really good." Peggy and Gina both laughed.

Chapter Thirty-One

On the last day of their vacation in Vermont, Shane and Gina took a little drive in the morning. They then spent the rest of the day walking around, enjoying the scenery near the Scenic View Inn. Gina took many photos on that last day. Many of them were of Paul and Peggy who were now not just considered inn keepers but special friends in their hearts.

Shane asked Paul, "Was it a tough decision for you to leave Atlanta and end up buying this inn in Vermont?"

Paul thought for a minute before saying, "It was a very tough decision. I had a high-paying job in Atlanta and we had no idea if we could make a go of it here. Peggy was concerned. I could see it in her eyes. We talked and talked about it for weeks. Finally, we decided that we would give it a try and if it didn't work out, we would go back to Atlanta. Shane, moving here was the best decision we ever made."

"I would imagine that you aren't as financially secure as you were in the city," Shane wanted to know.

Again, Paul gave it a minute or two before he said anything. Paul was not one to start talking before he knew exactly what he wanted to say. He put his arm around Shane as they were standing on the front porch. He pointed to the horizon and said, "Just look at that view. There is nothing like that in Atlanta."

Shane smiled at Paul and said to him, "I really understand now. I really understand."

It was about nearly the same time that Gina and Peggy were sitting in some comfortable chairs inside the inn. Gina said, "I'm going to miss chatting with you, Peggy. Tomorrow morning, Shane and I will be heading back to Kansas."

Peggy told Gina that she was going to miss her too. Peggy said, "I see so many people come here and look at the scenery and then head back to where they came from. Paul and I decided that we didn't want to put up with the hustle and bustle of the big city anymore. Moving here was a tough decision, but we know we made the right choice."

"You and Paul seem so at peace here and you give your guests such pleasant memories," Gina said.

Shane and Gina decided to get together and take one last walk around the property. They were sitting beneath some trees, having a little picnic lunch that was prepared by Peggy. Gina said, "Shane, if we didn't live in Kansas, would you like to live here?"

Shane looked off into the distance for a little while, seeming to take after Paul in not saying anything until he first thought it out. Shane finally nodded his head and said to Gina, "I could really imagine living here. Just look at the scenery. These autumn colors are fantastic. It gives you a feeling that you are meant to be here."

Gina smiled, as she took his hand in hers.

They finished their lunch and did some more walking around. It was a big change for them seeing the beautiful mountains here. They were used to the plains of Kansas. Change, Kansas was their home now and it seemed like the mention of Change was pulling them back to it. They both thought, we *met each other in Change, Kansas and we will never forget that first day that we met in the park.* Their thoughts brought smiles to their faces, as they looked at each other and sealed their love with a kiss.

The afternoon was ending and it was now early evening. On the front porch of the inn sat Shane, Gina, Paul, and Peggy rocking back and forth in the rocking chairs that lined the front porch. They were chatting as Gina was watching the sun lower in the western sky. It was just about to go behind the mountains, when the sky lit up in a brilliance of red. Gina said, "Oh my God everyone – just look at that sunset!" They all lifted their heads up to take a look. Shane and Gina were in awe as Paul and Peggy looked at them and smiled.

"Now, can you understand why we made this our home?" Paul said. "Do you see anything like that in Change, Kansas? I know we never did in Atlanta."

"That is amazing; I've never seen anything so beautiful," Shane said. Gina had the camera clicking, as she got shot after shot of the spectacular sunset.

It was well past dark and deep into the night when Gina said, "We better get to bed, Shane. It is going to be a long day for us tomorrow." Shane agreed as they stood up. Paul and Peggy sat there a little while longer but both told them to sleep well and they let them know how much they enjoyed having them as guests.

They did have a good sleep but got up early in the morning and hugged Paul and Peggy before heading back toward the airport. Arriving at the airport, they turned in the rental car and waited for the flight to Boston. The connecting flight would take them back to Kansas. Sitting in the terminal, Shane asked Gina, "Did you have a good time, honey?"

Gina looked at him with a smile on her face and said, "It was the best of times; I loved every minute of it."

Chapter Thirty-Two

Everyone was glad to see them back in Change, Kansas. Shane and Gina shared their experiences on the trip with everyone. It is nice going on a vacation, but it is also nice to get back home and be with all of your friends. Everyone here was so happy. So much love covered the city of Change, Kansas. Days back turned into weeks and then months. Shane and Gina often talked about the time they spent in Vermont.

Years ticked by slowly and the Donaldson's were starting a family. Gina had twin boys on the sixth year of their marriage. No couple could have been more proud than Shane and Gina. It seemed that their lives were now complete. Gina didn't want to work while the children were so young, so she left the diner. Betty understood and wished Gina well and told her that if she ever wanted to come back to work, she was welcome. Shane said, "Everything will be alright. We have some money in the bank and I'll be able to get plenty of overtime." Gina was in seventh heaven. She had often dreamed of the day when she and Shane would have children.

The children grew fast and every night when Shane came home from work, he gave all of the attention that he could to his twin boys. Cameron and Tyler brought many smiles to the faces of Shane and Gina. As soon as the boys were old enough to walk, Shane would have them out in the backyard playing. Gina often looked out of the kitchen window and thought of how many wonderful years she had shared with Shane. He was the man of her dreams. They had been married years now and she could honestly say that they had never fought once – a far cry from when Terry and she fought every day. She said to herself, *Terry, you were never a man. Men don't beat women. Shane is a man – a kind, caring, and loving man.*

The kids grew at a fast rate and before Shane and Gina knew it, they were attending school. Already in school, it gave Gina the chance to work some at the diner. Betty was glad to have her back. She let Gina flex her schedule so that she could be at any activities that the boys were attending. Often times, there were scheduled events and she was concerned that Shane had to work. She knew that Bill needed Shane there, as business was growing for Bill. Bill was best friends with Shane and Gina. He had done so much for them.

When the boys turned ten years old, it was a happy time for Shane and Gina. They threw a big party for them and invited many of their friends. Reverend Tillman stopped by and wished the boys a happy birthday. The reverend asked, "How is everything going with both of you?" Gina said that they had never been happier. The reverend smiled and said, "The two of you are the ideal couple."

For some reason, as Gina was cleaning up, she felt very dizzy. Shane noticed and said, "Are you alright, honey?"

"Yes, I'm fine. I just felt a little dizzy for a second," she said. "I guess it must be all of the excitement."

Shane helped her finish cleaning up and the two of them sat on the living room sofa and cuddled for the rest of the day. Cameron and Tyler teased them for looking like they were just starting to date. Shane said, "If you boys don't stop it right now, we may have to send you to bed early." They both laughed because they knew Shane was just kidding.

It was several months after the birthday party when Shane and the boys were out in the backyard tossing around a football that Cameron asked, "Is there something wrong with mommy?"

"I don't think so Cameron. Why do you ask?" Shane questioned him.

"I saw her in the kitchen yesterday waving her arms and talking to herself. It just seemed strange for mommy to act that way."

Tyler then replied, "I noticed her the other day looking out of the kitchen window and yelling for the kids to get out of the yard. Daddy, when I looked out, no one was there. What's wrong daddy?"

Shane stopped tossing the ball and said, "Come here, kids." As they all gathered around and sat on the grass, Shane wanted to know more.

They told Shane that they didn't know much more, but a few times, mommy just didn't seem like herself. He said, "I'll have a talk with her and see if she is feeling ok." The boys and Shane went back to playing ball, but Shane felt in his heart that something wasn't right. He knew that the boys spent more time with Gina and maybe there was something that he wasn't noticing. When they all went back inside, Gina was fast asleep on the living room sofa. Shane told the boys to let her sleep and he would talk with her later. Gina slept for the longest time and it was well past dark when she finally woke up. Shane said, "How are you feeling, honey? Is everything alright?"

"Yes, I'm feeling fine. I just had a little headache, so I thought I would take a nap," Gina said.

Shane smiled and said, "I love you, Gina. I love you very much."

Gina came over to Shane and said, "I love you very much too. You are the love of my life, Shane Williams."

Shane looked puzzled and replied, "Our name isn't Williams, honey. It is Donaldson."

"I don't know why I said that. Weird isn't it?" Gina said.

Shane thought to himself, *I'll have to keep an eye on Gina and see if I notice any strange behavior.*

It was about a week or two later while they were having dinner that Gina jumped up from the table and yelled, "You girls better behave yourselves in school! I got a call today."

Shane looked at Gina and said, "You mean the boys, don't you?"

"That's what I said," Gina replied.

Shane and the boys just looked at each other. Something was wrong. Shane didn't know what, but he knew that he had to have a talk with the family doctor. He made an appointment and wanted to talk to the doctor without Gina being along. It was made for two days later. Shane explained what had been going on with Gina. Dr. Tate said, "I'll have to examine her and send her for some tests. We'll get to the bottom of this. Don't worry, Shane." Shane made an appointment for Gina to come in and see the doctor.

Dr. Tate wanted to know if Gina had been feeling well. Gina said, "Sometimes, I feel kind of tired for no reason. I've also felt dizziness and have some headaches. It seems like they are getting worse." Dr. Tate told her that Shane had been worried about her. He did an examination and scheduled some tests for her. She would be getting blood tests and an MRI.

The tests were done and it was soon after that Dr. Tate called and said he had to see Shane and Gina in his office the first thing on the following morning. When they arrived at the office, both of them were prepared to hear the worst. Dr. Tate invited them into his office, not the examination room. It was a bad sign for Shane and Gina. He laid some papers down on his desk and looked so serious. "How are you feeling today, Gina?" he asked.

"I feel pretty good but I'm scared that you have some bad news," she said.

He nodded his head and told her that it was bad news. The MRI showed a large tumor in her brain. "Is it cancer?" Shane asked.

"By the size of it, I'm pretty sure it is. I've never seen one this large that wasn't," Dr. Tate replied. "You will have to go into the hospital, Gina, and have a biopsy done."

Gina arrived at the hospital the next day. They shaved her head where the procedure would be done. She was sedated and a small hole was drilled into her skull. A needle was inserted to get some tissue from the tumor to be used in the biopsy. It was only a short time when they got the news back. It was cancerous. They sat in Dr. Tate's office when Shane asked, "Is it operable?"

Dr. Tate shook his head and replied, "It's large and widespread. You have stage 4 cancer."

"How long do I have to live?" Gina said.

He told them that with proper treatment, Gina could live six months or a little more. Gina started to cry. She couldn't believe this was happening. Shane held her, as Dr. Tate gave her all of the options that were available to her. She would be going on chemotherapy right away.

Chapter Thirty-Three

Cameron and Tyler were outside playing with the neighbor's children when Shane and Gina pulled into the driveway. Gina looked at them as they walked slowly up to her. She had tears in her eyes. It was horrible news that she was going to have to tell them. Shane and Gina delayed giving them the bad news, but now it was time. They had to hear it.

Shane said, "Let's go into the living room, boys. There is something that mom and I have to talk to you about." Gina was walking slower and held onto Shane as they entered the front door of the house. Sitting in the living room, everyone just sat silent for the longest time. Shane and Gina were both thinking to themselves. Finally, Shane spoke first. "Boys, your mommy is very sick."

"You are going to get better, aren't you mommy?" asked Cameron. Gina held out her arms and the boys came to her. She hugged them and kept saying over and over how much she loved them.

Finally, Gina let go of them and they sat back down. She said, "I have brain cancer boys. That is why lately I have had dizziness, severe headaches, weakness, and some hallucinations. The tumor in my brain is very large and inoperable. I'm not going to get better. It will get worse, and at a very rapid rate. The doctors have given me at the most six months to live."

The boys burst out in tears and were screaming, "No, no, no! This can't happen! We love you mommy!"

Gina somehow managed to get a smile on her face and said, "I love you too, boys. That will never change. I do need something from you, though."

"What mommy? We will do anything?" Tyler said.

"I will be spending much time in and out of the hospital. I need you to do what you can to make things easier for your daddy and myself," said Gina.

"We will mommy. We'll do anything," Cameron said.

The next few weeks were very tough. The chemotherapy was taking a toll on Gina's body. Her hair was falling out and she was almost constantly vomiting. She laid in bed wondering if it was worth getting the chemotherapy, because she knew that she was going to die anyway. How could she tell Shane and the boys that she didn't want to take treatments anymore? How would they react? Could a miracle happen? Could she somehow survive all of this? Could God step in and help her?

Gina was lying in bed one evening – very weak from the latest treatments. She said, "Shane, we have to talk."

He came to her and sat on the edge of the bed. "What is it honey?" he wanted to know.

"Chemotherapy isn't helping much, Shane," she said.

"I know, honey that it is very hard on you. The doctors are trying to prolong your life for as long as they can," Shane replied.

"Would you want to prolong your life, if you were like this?" Gina said.

He shook his head no and asked her what she wanted to do. She said, "I want to stop the treatments and live what time I have left as best as I can."

"I understand, honey, but if you stop the treatments, you will have less time with me and the boys," he said.

"I know, but at least it will be more quality time. I want the time we have left to be special," she said.

"I love you, Gina Donaldson." They hugged and hugged and knew that Gina had to spend her last days in the way she wished.

Shane took the boys to the neighbors' for a little while. They asked how Gina was doing and Shane just shook his head. He said, "I just need some time alone for a little while. Would you mind watching the boys?" They said that they would be glad to do it. They also told Shane that if there was anything they could do, just let them know.

"Thanks, you two are so kind," Shane said.

Shane took a drive to the church and walked inside to pray. Reverend Tillman just happened to be there and saw Shane walk in. "How is Gina doing, Shane?" he asked.

"She isn't doing well, reverend," Shane responded. "She wants to stop the chemotherapy. I know it is her choice, but I want to keep her with me as long as possible. Do you think I'm wrong for feeling that way?"

"No, Shane, it is a natural feeling not to want to let go of someone you love so much. You and Gina have had many happy years together. Now, you have two wonderful boys. Life sometimes gives us a terrible blow, but God has made His choice for whatever reason He has," Reverend Tillman said.

"I want to talk to God. Do you think He will come to me?" Shane said.

The reverend said, "Give it a try, Shane. I know He hears you." Reverend Tillman walked away, leaving Shane to himself.

Shane was kneeling at the front of the church. He spoke quietly but clearly. He knew just what he wanted to say. "God, you have saved me from the depression of the death of my first wife. I never thought I could love again, but you led me to Gina. She is the finest woman that anyone could ever want. She made me love and smile again. Our life together was full of happiness and laughter. I don't understand why you are taking her from me at such an early age. Talk to me, God. Let me know. I don't understand. I love her, God. I love her very much."

Unclasping his hands and opening his eyes, Shane looked upward toward heaven. He was hoping that God would appear before him, like He did so many times as He was sending him on his journey to walk to Kansas. He didn't appear. Why was God ignoring him? He needed God now! "Please come to me!" he pleaded.

Shane went back home and walked into the bedroom. "We'll tell them tomorrow of your decision, honey."

Gina smiled at him and said, "I knew you would understand. Where were you?"

"I went to the church for a little while. I needed to speak to God," Shane said. Shane went next door and got the boys. He said, "I need you to do everything you can for mommy. Do you understand me?"

They nodded their heads yes. "She is going to go off of her treatments. She wants her final days on this earth to be the best they can be. So, we have to show her as much love as we can. She may act strange at times and say things that make no sense, but remember, that is the brain tumor."

Cameron and Tyler were so good to Gina. Every morning, they would come in and hug Gina and tell her how much they loved her. They would sit on the bed and talk to their mommy about all of the good times they had together. Gina loved both of them so much. She said to them, "Are you scared, boys?"

They both nodded yes and she could see the tears welling up inside their eyes. Gina added, "Don't cry, boys. It is God's wish that I go to Him."

"I hate God. I don't want to go to church anymore," Tyler said.

"Come here, Tyler. Don't ever think or say that. God knows what He is doing. He always has a reason for what

He does. Something good will come out of this. Maybe He has a plan for you boys, or maybe He has one for daddy. Be strong for me, boys," Gina said.

Cameron and Tyler spent much time talking between themselves of how hard it was seeing their mommy so sick. Shane knew that he had to spend more time with Gina. He asked Bill if he could take some time off. Bill needed Shane on the job, but he also knew that family came first. Shane and Gina had quite a bit of money in the bank. They would be fine financially for a few months. It was turning into the quality time that Gina wanted. It seemed that she was feeling better since the treatments had stopped. Dr. Tate did call Shane every now and then, wanting to know how Gina felt. Shane always told Dr. Tate that she was feeling as good as could be expected. Dr. Tate said, "Shane, if there is anything that I can do, please let me know." Shane thanked him for being so kind.

About one month after the treatments stopped, Shane noticed that oftentimes, Gina would just stare off into space. Her speech was getting more slurred. She was going down in weight. Every day, the boys and Shane spent as much time with her as they possibly could. Shane was amazed at how often Gina was smiling. Shane said, "You look happy today, Gina."

"I'm so happy that you are off work and spending so much time with me. How are the boys holding up?" she asked.

Shane hugged her and said, "I love spending time with you. I always have. As for the boys, it is hard on them, but they are doing the best they can."

"Cameron and Tyler are such good boys. They are in here so much – telling me how much they love me. How could anyone not love them?" she said.

Chapter Thirty-Four

Betty and Jim came to see Gina often. Gina loved Betty and the feeling was mutual. Gina had worked for Joe and Betty for a long time. Every time they talked, Gina always said how much she loved Joe and how nice Joe was to her. It was hard on Gina when Joe died so suddenly. She was there for Betty – doing everything that she possibly could. Now, it was Betty's turn, but there wasn't much she could do except talk and give Gina some memories to hold onto. Gina always thanked Betty for coming. The other waitresses at the diner also often came by and told Gina how much they missed her.

Shane often just sat by himself and did much thinking. His first wife had died so suddenly. He often wished that he could have spent more time with her. Now, Gina was dying a slow death. He wondered to himself, *what was worse – having someone you love die suddenly or having him or her die a slow death?* It was taking a toll on Shane – seeing the woman he loved and knowing that any day she could die. He still stayed strong, especially around the boys. They seemed to get their strength from Shane. Shane had always wished that he would be the first one to die but it wasn't to be.

Gina was talking to him one evening and said, "Shane, we have to make some final plans. I want to be cremated and I want you to take my ashes back to Vermont and spread them on that place behind the rock where we made love on the pile of leaves. Do you remember when we did that?"

Shane gave a little laugh and said, "How could I ever forget that?! That was special. I remember when you asked Paul if he ever made love on a pile of leaves. He was so embarrassed." Shane and Gina were both laughing. Shane once again saw the beauty in Gina that he hadn't been seeing much of lately. Shane wanted to know how she had been feeling of late. She told Shane that she just felt the time was getting near. Gina had no idea of how much longer she had to live but she knew the end was nearing.

The cancer was spreading to other parts of Gina's body. She was in constant pain and was taking the strongest prescription pain killers that she could. Often, she was silent, spoke very little and just stared into space. Shane spent every moment he could holding onto Gina's hands and several times, got her to smile. He now realized that it was best that Becky died the way she did. He could not have possibly imagined how it was to see someone you love die so slowly. Gina was sleeping more and more and he realized that it was now just a matter of days before his wife Gina would be in heaven.

Shane wouldn't leave her side during those last days. The boys would bring him something to eat and they hugged Shane often. They would lean over and kiss Gina on the cheek and say, "We love you, mommy. We love you so much."

Shane never realized that the boys could stay so strong through this ordeal. Gina woke up one morning and said to Shane, "Hold me, honey. Please hold me."

Shane held her in his arms as he said, "I love you, Gina Donaldson!"

Gina seemed like she had a new life in her. She held Shane tight – looking at him and giving him a smile. Gina said, "I love you, Shane Donaldson, but it is time for me to go." Gina closed her eyes and fell limp in Shane's arms.

Shane just held onto her and cried and cried. The boys walked into the room and Shane said, "She is gone now. She will be looking down on you boys from heaven." Shane and the boys hugged.

Each of the boys held Gina's hand, kissed her on the cheek, and said, "I love you, mommy." Shane was so proud of his boys. He knew how much they loved their mommy. Life was going to be different now.

"She is out of pain now," Shane said as he looked at Cameron and Tyler. "Your mommy's wish is to be cremated and she wants me to take her ashes to Vermont and spread them in a special place of ours."

Tyler was rubbing Gina's face with tears running down his cheeks. Tyler said, "Daddy, you really loved mommy very much, didn't you?"

"Yes, son. I did love her very much."

Shane called the authorities and Gina's body was taken to the funeral home. Shane made the final arrangements. He then sent an email to Paul and Peggy in Vermont and told them of what had happened. He wanted to come back to the inn and stay for a few days. Peggy emailed him back and said they would be expecting him and how sorry Paul and her were to hear the news. Shane made arrangements for the neighbors to take care of the kids for a while. They were more than glad to do it.

It seemed like everyone in Change, Kansas was at the funeral. So many tears were flowing. Betty couldn't control her emotions. Shane told her how much Gina loved her and Joe. "You both had a big impact on her life," Shane said.

"She had a big influence in our lives too," replied Betty.

Gina was cremated as per her wishes. Shane held the urn containing Gina's ashes. He could no longer control himself. He hadn't cried that much in his life. The last few months had been more of a strain on him than he realized. He said goodbye to the boys and told them to be good. He knew that they would, but he just had to say it anyway. He guessed that was what a parent was supposed to do. Looking at the urn, he smiled and said, "You would have said the same thing to the boys, and you know it."

As he walked into the Scenic View Inn in Vermont, Paul and Peggy hugged him and told Shane how sorry they were. Paul said, "Of all the people that have visited here since we bought this place, you and Gina were the ones that we liked the most."

Shane told Paul and Peggy of Gina's final wishes. Peggy said that she thought it was so sweet. "We have your room ready. Would you like to get some sleep?" Peggy said.

"Yes, I'm very tired," said Shane. "Tomorrow is going to be a tough day on me."

Chapter Thirty-Five

The next morning, Shane came down for breakfast but hardly said a word. It was a long time ago that Shane and Gina had sat at this very table and had breakfast. Those were happy times in their lives. Peggy was pouring some more coffee for Shane, but he hardly noticed. His mind was elsewhere and she knew it. Peggy knew that Shane was hurting inside. He had two special women in his life. Many people don't even get one that they love as much as he loved Becky and Gina. He got up from the table and went to his room to get the urn containing Gina's ashes. He held it for the longest time – picturing Gina in his mind. It was many years ago that they were in this room, talking about how beautiful the scenery was here. He smiled at those memories. Shane knew that he would never forget the two women in his life that brought him so much happiness.

Shane turned around and walked downstairs. Paul was sitting on the front porch when he walked outside and said good morning to Shane. Shane said, "I have to walk to where I'm going to spread the ashes."

"It is miles to that spot," Paul said. "Shane, are you sure you don't want to drive to the trail?" Shane told him no. He had to walk. It was how they met for the first time and it would be how they depart. Shane told Paul not to worry if he didn't get back until late or didn't get back at all that night. He needed time to think and there couldn't be a nicer place than the mountains of Vermont to do it.

Shane was walking down a country road in Vermont. To where he needed to get was about an eleven-mile walk. He knew that walking was the way he had to do this. After all, that was the way that Shane and Gina had met. He knew that Gina would be looking down on him – smiling that he chose to pay tribute to her in this way. It was a little late in the morning when he came to the trail that led off of the highway. It had been a long time, but it looked much like it did years ago. Shane walked up the trail and looked at the views. He remembered Gina taking many photos of that day long ago. It was about half an hour walking the trail when he spotted the large rock. *There it is,* he thought.

Shane walked to the rock and looked behind it. It was here that Shane and Gina had made love on a pile of leaves. Shane sat the urn down near a tree and started to gather leaves again. He made the pile as nearly as he could from memory. He pressed his hand down on the leaves – just like he did before. Picking up the urn, he said, "Your wish has come true, Gina. You are now back to one of our favorite spots. It was here that we made love. I remember making love to you so many times. Each time was just as special as the time before. I remember saying once in Hawaii that you were going to kill me someday." He smiled, turned around and looked at the pile of leaves. He took the urn and sprinkled the ashes over that leaf pile. *Your final resting place, my love,* he thought.

Shane went to the nearest tree and sat down – leaning against it. He just looked at the pile of leaves and let his life with Gina flash before him. He remembered the day they first met in the park. It had been a long journey by both of them. God knew that they were meant for each other. He had to wonder why God didn't answer him and save Gina from the brain cancer that eventually killed her. He spent a lot of time leaning against that tree – staring at the leaves and wondering why her life had to end. She was so full of life only a few months ago. People just never know when they will be called to heaven. Shane spoke to himself, "I loved every minute of my life with you, Gina – every minute." He took the urn and leaned it against the rock. "Rest in peace, Princess," were his final words.

He left that spot and started his walk back to the inn. Most of the way back, he had tears in his eyes. They were mixed tears. Some of them were tears of sorrow and others were tears of joy, as he thought back to what they had done together. It was tough to see her health deteriorate the last few months, and much of the time, she was in terrible pain. *No one should have to go through such agony,* he thought. He continued walking and approached the Scenic View Inn just as darkness fell over the mountains. He looked up to see Paul and Peggy sitting on the front porch. Peggy looked at Shane and said, "Are you alright, Shane?"

Shane just nodded and sat down in one of the chairs. "Bad things just shouldn't happen to good people," he said. Paul and Peggy knew what he meant. Gina was a sweet and lovely person.

"People worry about many things in their lives. They worry about their jobs, their houses, their cars. None of them mean anything. It is the people they love that matters," Shane said.

"You are so right, Shane," Paul said. "I don't know what I would do if anything happened to Peggy."

"Love each other like every day is your last, for you never know when it will be," Shane told them. Peggy was getting so emotional. She could see that Shane was hurting inside. Peggy wished that there was something she could do to make him feel better. However, she knew that it would take time. Shane wouldn't get over this for many months – maybe years.

Peggy went inside the inn and Paul and Shane were on the front porch by themselves. They were sitting in the dark and looking into a star-filled sky. Shane said, "You know, Paul, it sure is pretty here."

"I know it is," Paul replied. "Shane, it is so peaceful. We will never get rich here, but Peggy and I are stress-free."

Shane nodded his head yes, because he knew exactly what Paul was getting at. Shane said, "Paul, can I ask you something?"

Paul gestured that it was alright to do so. Shane said, "If I moved to this area, would I be able to find work?"

Paul wanted to know, "What kind of work are you looking for?"

"Landscaping, handyman work – something where I can work with my hands," Shane said. "I'm not the type of person that wants to sit behind a desk all day. I'm not a suit and tie type man, as you've probably already figured."

Paul told Shane that he and Peggy had been talking about hiring someone to do a lot of the work around there. "Would you be interested?" Paul wanted to know.

"I really would," was Shane's answer.

"One thing is that I couldn't pay you much," Paul said.

Shane advised him that a big paycheck wasn't the most important thing in his life right now. Shane figured that this would be a nice place to raise Cameron and Tyler. "When are you planning on moving, Shane?" Paul asked.

Shane told him that it wouldn't be long. He would have to go back to Change, Kansas and get his affairs in order. He would put the house up for sale soon and if he had to rent it out for a while before it sold, he could do that. Peggy walked out on the front porch and immediately, Paul said to her, "What would you think of us hiring Shane as our handyman?"

"Are you serious? I think that would be fantastic," Peggy said.

Paul replied, "Shane Donaldson, you're hired." They all laughed and hugged.

Shane stayed a couple of more days. He just needed some time to relax. He had been under so much stress lately. When Shane left to go back to Kansas, he told Paul that he would call him when he got back and try to give him a date as to when he could be back in Vermont.

Chapter Thirty-Six

Back in Change, Shane took the boys aside and told them that he was thinking of moving to Vermont. He wanted to know how they felt about it. Shane showed them many photos that Gina had taken on their vacation there years ago. Cameron said, "It looks like a beautiful place."

Shane told them that it was and he was sure they would like it there. "Daddy, does this have anything to do with the fact that you spread mommy's ashes there?" Tyler asked. Shane couldn't deny that Gina was in his mind.

Shane hugged the boys and they all went off to bed. Shane slept well that night, but he woke up sometime in the middle of the night. It took him a second to clear his eyes. Then, he saw God sitting on the edge of his bed. God said, "I guess you are probably surprised to see me, aren't you?"

Shane nodded his head yes and then asked, "Why didn't you save Gina?"

God knew that Shane was going to ask that question. God said, "Shane, you and Gina had many years together. It wasn't to be that she would be cured. It was time for her to go to heaven." God and Shane talked for a little while before God said, "There is something else in your plans, Shane." Shane wanted to know what it was, but God only said, "You will know what it is and you will know when to do it, when the time comes." Shane tried to keep Him from leaving before he found out more, but God disappeared into the night.

Shane wondered what God meant. Surely, he wouldn't want him to walk across the country again. It sounded like God wanted him to figure it out for himself. God can lead you and advise you, but the final decisions are to be made by you. Shane thought about it a lot of the time during the next few weeks, as he and the boys were cleaning out the house, garage and storage shed. It was a lot of work, but it was something that had to be done. Shane was selling off much of the furniture because when he moved to Vermont, he would be living in a guest house that was on the Scenic View Inn property. Paul had said the guest house had been unused for a few years and was fully furnished.

Shane already had someone that wanted to rent the house. They were a younger couple that just moved into town and they just loved the house and property. The rental was set up through a property management company, so the rent could be collected by them and they could take care of any repairs or concerns the new tenants would have about the house. Shane welcomed the couple into the house and told them that he wished they would be as happy there as he and his wife had been.

The car was packed up and they spent one night in a hotel before they would start the long drive to Vermont. Bill was so sorry to see Shane go. He said, "I'm really going to miss you, but I can understand why you want to go."

Shane thanked Bill for everything and then walked over to the diner to see Betty. She was in the back office doing some paperwork when Shane walked in. One of the waitresses told her Shane wanted to see her before he left town. Betty said, "I'm so sorry about what has happened, Shane. Gina was so loved here."

"I know she was, Betty. She loved you and Joe so much. It's a tough time right now, but I think once we get to Vermont, we'll get our lives back in order. Thank you for everything you have done for us," Shane said.

It was early the next morning when Shane and the boys pulled out of town. Shane told them that he loved this place, but it was time to get away now. Cameron asked his dad if he would ever get married again. Shane said, "I don't know, son. When Becky died, I never thought I would, but then I met your mom and we fell instantly in love." Shane thought about it during the drive. He knew if he ever did get married again, it wouldn't be for a long time. He had two marriages and two tragic endings. He couldn't possibly imagine again going through what he had gone through twice in his life. If it wasn't for the boys, Shane didn't think he would have made it this time without a total emotional breakdown.

Shane knew this was going to be a long trip and that he would have to stay over a couple of nights. It was on the third day of driving that he pulled the car into the driveway of the Scenic View Inn. Paul and Peggy welcomed all of them and told Shane that he had two fine-looking boys. Shane said, "Yes, they got their good looks from their mother."

Everyone laughed – including the boys. Paul gave Shane the key to the guest house and said, "We hope that it is satisfactory to all of you."

As she looked at the boys, Peggy asked, "How do you like the mountains?"

"It is so beautiful. I'm sure we are going to like it here," Cameron said.

Shane said, "We're pretty tired from traveling. I think we'll get settled in and get a little sleep."

Shane woke up first and decided to let the boys sleep for a little while longer. He walked around to the front porch and saw Paul sitting outside. He walked up to Paul and said, "Would you like to show me around the place tomorrow and let me know what you would like me to work on?"

"I'd be glad to, Shane. I'm sure you will do a good job for us." Paul added, "You'll have to get the boys registered for school. Peggy will take you there and help you out. The school bus will stop right at the end of the driveway."

Shane thanked him and said, "I guess I'll wake up the boys, and then we're going to go to the store and buy some groceries."

With the shopping done, it was time for Shane to make the boys some dinner. He said, "Peggy and I are going to get you boys registered for school tomorrow." Shane heard a groan coming from both of the boys. "Now, you know you have to go to school," said Shane. "Your mother would want you boys to get a good education."

The months that followed were very good. Shane loved his job of working as the handyman. He didn't have any set hours and could flex them any way that he wanted, as long as the work got done. Paul was sure that he would never run out of work. The boys were well adjusted to school and even looked forward to going. It was on a Sunday after church that Shane asked the boys if they wanted to go fishing. They both were so excited when Shane walked into the room carrying two fishing poles. They spent that day fishing and talking. Actually, the boys did more talking than fishing, but that was alright with Shane. At least they were spending a day together. Cameron looked out over the lake and said, "Daddy, will you take us to the spot where you spread mommy's ashes?"

"I'd be glad to boys. What do you say we go right now?"

Shane drove them to the spot where the trail led up a long hill. Several times, the boys looked at the view and said, "I remember this view in one of mommy's photos!" Shane agreed with them that it was so pretty. Tyler said, "I'm so glad we moved to the mountains. I love it here." Shane couldn't argue about that. It really was beautiful.

Soon, they came to the large rock that Shane and Gina made love behind. They walked behind it and Shane said,

"This is the spot, boys. Your mother and I loved it here."
The boys just looked at each other and kind of shrugged
their shoulders. Shane knew that the boys didn't see
anything special about this spot; however, Shane couldn't
tell the whole story. He had to keep some secrets to himself.

As they were walking back to the car, both of the boys
said, "Thank you, daddy. We love mommy so much."

Shane smiled and told them that he did too. It was a
good Sunday – the best they had together since moving to
Vermont.

Chapter Thirty-Seven

Everything was going very well for the Donaldson family in their new home. The boys loved the mountains and spending time in the forest. Shane thought they were getting to be little mountain men. Almost every week, they took a hike somewhere. The boys loved to just sit on a rock somewhere or by a tree and take in the scenery. Both of them were getting very good at skipping rocks across the surface of a lake.

A chill in the air came early in the fall to the mountains. The leaves were so beautiful and when they fell off, Shane had to keep the grounds of the inn cleaned up. Paul said to him, "It's quite a job, isn't it Shane?" Shane agreed but told him it was the greatest time of the year. Paul had to agree with him on that one. Paul said, "Soon you will see snow covering the mountains. I'm sure you will want to get a couple of sleds for the boys. I know they will love sliding down the hills."

Shane woke up early one morning to see the first snow of the year. It wasn't deep at all, but the beauty of the snow hanging on the trees was a sight to behold. Shane woke up the boys and the first thing they wanted to do was to go out and play in it. Shane, the boys, and Paul all joined in to have a snowball fight. Peggy was just watching them and laughing. When they were finished, she said, "It looks now like I have four little boys to watch out for." Paul and Shane just laughed and enjoyed playing with the boys so much.

It was getting colder almost every morning and even some afternoons. Shane was so glad that he decided to leave Change, Kansas – even though he loved it there. He just thought that moving would be easier on him after Gina's death. He often felt that he was a very lucky man to have loved twice. Many people don't get the chance to have a true love once. *God has been good to me,* he thought. That thought got him to wondering. What did God mean when He said that He had other plans for him? Nothing had happened in months that would signal to him that he needed to do something. God did tell him that he would know when the time came; however, Shane did wonder and wonder when it would happen. What would it be? Would it involve the boys? There were so many questions that he had, but he knew God always had a reason.

It was almost a year later when Paul was watching the news on TV that he saw a young child – who did not live to far away – had a brain tumor. The news program also stated that it was inoperable. The boy was in much pain, and the hospital bills were a burden to the parents. Shane asked Paul if he knew the people and Paul did say that he knew them a little bit, but not really well. Shane said, "I wonder if I talked to them, if it would help."

"If anyone could help them get through this, I know it would be you," he said. Paul got the phone number for the family and Shane gave them a call. Shane told them that he saw on the news that their son was very sick. He told them that his wife Gina had died of brain cancer and he knew how devastating it could be. They said they would like to talk with Shane and listen to what he had to say. Shane hung up the phone and sat down in a living room chair. This is what God meant. He knew that maybe he could help someone else deal with what he had to deal with.

Shane arrived at their house later that day, after he had finished his work at the inn. They were a nice young couple named Steve and Sharon Winston. They welcomed him into the living room and they sat down and started to talk. Sharon said, "I can't believe this is happening to us."

"I know how you feel, Sharon. When the doctor told Gina and me that she had stage four brain cancer and it was inoperable, it felt like I was hit in the face with a sledge hammer. It was just total shock. I had no one to talk to, except the doctors, because no one in Change, Kansas had ever gone through what Gina was about to face," Shane said.

He continued, "When something like that happens, you feel you have to go with what the doctors recommend. Gina was on chemotherapy for quite some time. She was constantly crying and vomiting. Her hair was all gone. She knew that she was going to die anyway. One day, she told me she wanted to go off of the treatments. In my heart, I didn't want her to. I wanted to keep her with me, as long as possible. I finally realized I was only thinking of myself. Gina stopped the treatments because she realized: why go through such a horrible process when she knew she was going to die. It had to be her decision and I supported her."

Shane took a little time to regain his composure before he continued. "The last few weeks, she was racked with pain and did take pain killers. She had times when she just stared and times when she said things that didn't make any sense of reality. There were times when she wanted me to hold her. It was tough seeing someone who I loved die. My first wife died tragically in a car accident and was killed instantly. It was then that I wished I had more time with her. After dealing with Gina's illness, I realized that prolonging an illness, when you know what the final ending will be, isn't right. I feel sorry for both of you, because I know what you are going through."

"What do you think we should do, Shane?" Steve asked.

"I can't answer that. I can only tell you what it was like for me," Shane said. "It was tough to let go, but I knew in my heart it was the right decision."

"The doctors are sure he doesn't have much more time left," Sharon said. "It is so tough seeing him in pain."

"I know it is, Sharon. Believe me, I know it is. I know you will make the right decision for your son."

"Thank you, Shane, for coming by and talking with us. We had no one to talk this over with, except the doctors. I now see it through the eyes of someone who has actually been through this," Steve said.

"Talking with you is something that we really needed to do," Sharon said. "You should write a book. All we can find is medical books that are just technical mumbo jumbo. You could probably help many people realize what they will be going through in such a situation."

As Shane was leaving, he knew that what he said had an impact on Steve and Sharon. What would they do? He didn't know? It had to be their decision and their decision only. He felt so sorry for them, but he knew they loved talking with him about it. He now knew clearly just what God had planned for him. He wasn't a public speaker or a writer. What would he do from here? He needed some time to think about it.

Could he write a book? He didn't know. Maybe he could? Could he speak in public about Gina's death? What else could he do to help Steve and Sharon? So many questions were popping into his head as he was driving back to the inn. They needed help with their bills. Maybe he could do something to get some help for them. The next morning, Shane walked into the inn and talked with Paul. "Did you talk with Steve and Sharon?" Paul asked.

"Yes, I did and they really listened to what I had to say. Paul, they need some help financially. I was thinking about taking a day and going around door-to-door to try to get donations to pay for their son's medical bills."

"Here, Shane, let me write you out a check to get started." Paul handed it to him. It was a check for $500. Shane smiled and thanked Paul.

Shane was on the road the next morning going door-to-door and getting donations. He went to homes and businesses. No one turned him down. He was dead tired by the time he got home. All totaled, he had raised $58,128 to pay for the medical bills of Steve and Sharon's little boy. Shane went to the bank the next day and turned in everything he received. He then got a cashier's check made out to Steve and Sharon Winston. He saw on the news before he went to bed that Tommy Winston had died that day. Shane was in tears because he knew what Steve and Sharon had gone through. He looked up and said, "Thank you, God. It was time for him to go. Thank you for helping me understand. I know that I can make a difference. I can help someone who is going through what I did."

The next day, Shane pulled into the driveway of Steve and Sharon. He sat in the car for a while before going to the door. Sharon opened the door and gave Shane a big hug. Steve did likewise and invited Shane inside. Shane said, "I'm so sorry to hear about your son."

"Thanks, Shane. You had really made me and Sharon think a lot about what was going on. We realized that if we really loved Tommy, it was time to let him go. He is no longer in pain and is now in heaven," Steve said. Shane smiled and agreed with what Steve had just said. He remembered very well the pain that was racking Gina's body.

"You helped us greatly, Shane," Sharon said. "You need to help others. There are many like us. To hear it from someone who has gone through it is what people need."

Shane told them that he didn't know what he would do yet. He had been thinking a lot about it. He told them that

God had come to him after Gina's death and said that He had a plan for him. "I know now what that plan was: to help others like yourselves," said Shane. "You'll be hearing from me again but I have to go now. Before I go, I want to give you this check to help pay for some of the medical bills that you have been plagued with."

Steve and Sharon looked at it and couldn't believe their eyes. They both started to cry as Steve said, "This will help immensely. Bills have really been piling up. Thank you, Shane. Thank you very much and God bless you."

"A lot of people nearby were following Tommy's story on the news and they were all so glad to chip in," Shane explained. He left to go back to the inn, but he knew he would be talking with Steve and Sharon again.

Chapter Thirty-Eight

Shane spent much time in the next few months thinking about what he could do to help others. He did jot down a few ideas that he had for writing a book. He was also thinking about how to raise money to help other families that were in need. Shane felt that somehow, he needed to talk with other families and let them know the options and decisions that they had to make. When the word "cancer" is mentioned in a diagnosis, people's worlds can tumble down in a hurry. Combine the word "cancer" with "inoperable," and the world seems to have ended for them. When those words were mentioned to Shane and Gina, they both knew that their world would never be the same.

Shane continued to work around the Scenic View Inn. Paul and Peggy were so pleased with his work. He did a fantastic job for them. Peggy did mention to Paul one day that she had seen something different about Shane lately. Paul agreed with her and thought that the death of Tommy Winston had something to do with it. Paul said, "Shane brought a different meaning of life to Steve and Sharon. His words really were well received and he busted his tail to raise so much money for them. I think Shane is thinking of ways to help others in the same situation."

Paul didn't know it yet, but he was so right about Shane. Shane spent every evening on the computer putting down words about how life changed for him. The boys would often walk into the room and ask what he was doing.

Shane said, "Do you boys remember how much you loved your mommy and how hard it was watching her die a slow painful death?"

"It was very hard daddy, and I know how you kept our family together until the very end. I think about mommy every day – every single day," Cameron said.

Shane smiled and said, "I do too son, and that is one reason why I'm trying to write a book. We can't ever let mommy be forgotten and we need to do what we can to help other people." Shane talked with many people. He made calls and sent emails all over the country, asking questions about how he could get a foundation started.

He talked with rich people. He talked with poor people. He talked with everyone who would listen. The local news that followed Tommy Winston's bout with brain cancer heard what Shane had done for the family. They wanted to talk to Shane and do a story on the local news. He had a story to tell and people needed to hear it. Shane was nervous that he was getting so much attention. The news crew arrived and he had a great interview. When it aired on the evening news, it really touched people's hearts.

The story of what Shane had done for Steve and Sharon Winston made the national news by the end of the week. Shane just stared at the TV as the story was being aired. He was now being praised as a national hero. It was a few days later when Paul brought a large sack of mail back to the guest house. Shane said, "What is this?"

"Apparently, you made quite a hit with people all across America," replied Paul. "This is your mail."

Shane couldn't believe what he was reading as he looked through the letters he had received. He received donations from almost everyone. He was asked to visit certain people and speak to them. He knew he had no way of being able to talk to so many people across America. Every day the letters kept coming. Donations were piling up. He opened a bank account and deposited each of them.

Phone call after phone call was received by him every day. He had mentioned in the interview that he wanted to start a foundation for terminally ill people in honor of his wife, Gina. He had mentioned that he had no idea of how to get this done. One of the phone calls he received was to be on a national television talk show. He accepted the invitation from Jennifer Wilkins. It was her talk show that would tell the country of Shane and Gina's life. He was more nervous than ever, as she asked him question after question. Shane answered every one of them – straight-forward. One of Jennifer's last questions was, "Would you mind if we helped you get your foundation started?"

"No, I would appreciate any help I can get," Shane said.

Jennifer told Shane and the nationwide audience that she had contacted a lawyer friend of hers to get a foundation legally started. The lawyer came out and did some talking with Jennifer and Shane. He said, "Shane, with the help of Jennifer and some other friends, we have started in Gina's honor, The Gina Donaldson Foundation for the Terminally Ill. We are presenting this check today in the amount of five hundred thousand dollars."

Shane was shocked and then told of all the letters he had been receiving that contained cash and checks which he deposited in his local bank. "The total from many people across the country is in excess of two million dollars," said Shane. "This will be added to the foundation to help the terminally ill and their families."

Jennifer explained that Shane would have to spend some time getting the foundation off the ground and the lawyer wanted his input on just what he would like to see done with the money. He said, "Shane, this will be a nonprofit organization whose only purpose is to help people."

Shane was in tears on national television. He thanked Jennifer and her lawyer friend. He said, "This is an incredible honor and a fabulous tribute to Gina. I know she is looking down on us with a smile."

The foundation was getting off the ground, as Shane continued to work on his book. It would take him a year to get it just the way he wanted it. It was submitted and accepted immediately, probably because of all the attention he had been receiving. The book was flying off the shelves by the millions. He had book signings across the country. Shane set it up with the publisher so that ninety percent of the profits would go to the foundation. It was adding millions of dollars. Shane decided to keep ten percent to give him the money to send Cameron and Tyler to college and for him to live well the rest of his life. That ten percent was still making Shane a very wealthy man. Shane still wanted the quiet life of living in the mountains of Vermont. He had spent a lot of time away from the Scenic View Inn. Paul missed him, but totally understood. He was now back, and the foundation was being run by people who were very capable.

Shane – on occasion – had to travel to give speeches on what it was like to watch his wife die of brain cancer. He always told the truth. That was what people wanted to hear. The hardest part of what Shane did now was to visit hospitals and see children who were terminally ill. Shane never knew that there would be so many. He thought, *No child should die at such an early age.* He talked with many parents and told them of his experiences, but always left saying they were the ones that had to make the final decision. He received many letters thanking him.

He was answering as many of the letters as he could. He did realize that there was no possible way that he could answer all of them. The letters he received from people who had a terminally ill child always touched his heart deeply.

He did everything he could to answer those. It was several months later that he received a letter from Alabama, sent by Sylvia Chestnut. He looked at the return address for a few minutes. Shane knew that name from somewhere. It was coming back to him now. It must have been close to twenty-five years ago. He was walking across the northeast corner of Alabama and came to a farmer's market stand. It was run by a woman named Sylvia Chestnut. She had let him sleep in her home for the night and gave him a great dinner and a fabulous breakfast, before he started walking again on his journey. Sylvia gave a one hundred dollar donation made out to the foundation. She also wrote that she would like to see Shane again. Sylvia was planning a vacation and wanted to come and see Shane.

Shane smiled and said, "I'd like to see you again, Sylvia." He saw that she left a phone number in the letter. Shane felt kind of awkward calling a woman he hadn't seen in twenty-five years. A woman answered the phone.

"Sylvia, this is Shane Donaldson."

She told him hello. They talked for the longest time about when he spent the night there and what happened to Shane on his journey. Sylvia said, "I'd like to come to Vermont and see you, if you don't mind."

"I don't mind at all. I'd be glad to see you," Shane replied. Sylvia told him that she was so sorry about what she had heard about Gina.

"You must have loved her very much," Sylvia said. Shane told her that he did.

Chapter Thirty-Nine

It was a month later when Sylvia Chestnut arrived at the Scenic View Inn. Shane just happened to be doing some work on the front porch when she drove up. She got out of the car and looked around for a couple of minutes. The view to her was breathtaking. Shane looked at her and thought to himself: *Sylvia is still a very attractive woman.* "Hi, Sylvia," he said, as he stepped off of the porch and walked up to her. He gave her a kiss on the cheek and they gave each other a hug.

"It's been a long time," Sylvia said.

"Indeed it has," replied Shane. "You look very nice, Sylvia." They talked for a few minutes before Shane led Sylvia inside and introduced her to Paul and Peggy.

Sylvia got settled into the same room that Shane had stayed in a couple of times. Sylvia loved the peacefulness that the inn gave to her. She was sitting out on the front porch, just looking out over the mountains. Peggy came to the doorway and said, "Do you like it here, Sylvia?"

"Oh yes, the mountains are so beautiful," she said.

"How do you and Shane know each other?" Peggy said. Sylvia told Peggy the story of how Shane came to her farmer's market stand and how she let him sleep in her house for one night. Peggy was very interested and was sorry to hear that her husband died in the war.

Peggy told Sylvia that Shane and Gina had come to the inn one year on vacation and they both fell in love with the place. She told Sylvia that Shane came back to spread Gina's ashes somewhere on one of the trails. "Shane felt he had to get away from where he was living and it just so happened that we were looking for a handyman," explained Peggy. "The work was getting to be too much for Paul."

Peggy asked why Sylvia never got married again and Sylvia told her that she never met the right man. Sylvia said, "Shane is a nice man, isn't he?"

Peggy agreed and said, "It must have been awfully hard on him – having two of his wives die the way they did." Sylvia knew it had. Having her husband die changed her life forever.

Shane walked around the corner of the inn carrying a ladder. He said, "Are you two women talking about me?" They both laughed and told Shane that of course they were. He said, "My ears were burning and now I know why."

"Shane, I'm going to cook a very special dinner for you and the boys tonight," Sylvia said. Shane smiled and blushed. He could imagine what Peggy was thinking.

"I have more work to do before this day is over." he said. "I'll talk to both of you later." Peggy decided to come out on the porch and sit in one of the rocking chairs. She and Sylvia talked for the longest time. Peggy didn't say anything, but she was thinking of the time Shane and Gina came back to the inn and Gina asked Paul if he had ever made love on a pile of leaves. He was so embarrassed. It made her smile every time she had thought of that story.

"You'll have to excuse me, Sylvia. I have to get inside and start preparing dinner," Peggy said. So, I guess you will be in the guest house tonight having dinner with Shane."

"Yes, I will and I better start getting dinner ready for him too. I imagine he will be plenty hungry himself after a hard day's work," Sylvia said.

Peggy told her that she wished for her and Shane to have a good evening. Sylvia thought back to the time when she made him dinner in Alabama. That was so many years ago. When she had seen him walking away that day, she thought she would never see him again. She thought, *People just never know what life has in store for them.*

The boys came in the house first and said, "Hi, Sylvia."

"Hi, boys," she said. "Did you have a nice day?"

They said that they had. Sylvia wanted to know if Shane was almost done for the day. Cameron said that he was and would be inside in a few minutes. Sylvia had a fine meal prepared for them. Shane said, "Boys, whose cooking is better – mine or Sylvia's?" The boys couldn't control their laughter. They were cracking up.

"Stop it, dad," Tyler said. "We can't take it anymore!" Shane and Sylvia started to laugh right along with them. In a minute, Shane was just sitting there silent and remembering back to the day that Sylvia made dinner for him, years and years ago.

"Boys, will you do the dishes tonight while Sylvia and I go for a walk?" Shane asked. They were glad to do it. They both knew how hard things had been on their dad.

Shane and Sylvia took a long time walking around the grounds of the inn. Shane said, "I love it here, Sylvia. It really is a beautiful place. Just look at the views of the mountains!"

Sylvia turned around and smiled. She looked back at Shane and said, "I've decided to sell my home in Alabama. It's just gotten to be so much for me to handle by myself as I get older."

"You aren't an old woman, Sylvia. You still look young and attractive," Shane said.

"Thank you, but the years are starting to tick by," she replied. "I want an easier life now. I'm not sure where to settle down."

Shane knew what she was talking about. After all, he was in his fifties now. "How come you never remarried?" he asked.

She smiled and said, "I just never found the right man, or maybe I did and he walked away." Shane stopped in his tracks.

He looked at Sylvia and said, "I thought about it that day, when we were having breakfast. God had different plans for me then."

"I know that His plan was for you to meet Gina. I'm so glad that she made you happy, Shane. I know that you both had a wonderful life together. When I read your book, I could tell that she was the one for you," she said.

"We both know that God always knows what is best for us," Shane replied.

Sylvia nodded her head yes. Sylvia told him that she thought about him a lot for a few years. As the years went on, she didn't think about him as much. However, when she bought that book and read the story, she realized that she still had a flame in her heart. Shane and Sylvia continued to walk and chat about what had happened in their lives during the past twenty-five plus years. They both had a good life. Sylvia loved the life that she lived. She did get lonely at times, but she never was the one to just sit around.

It was on a Saturday when Sylvia packed a picnic lunch. Shane, Sylvia and the boys were heading out on a hike in the forest of the mountains of Vermont. It was such a beautiful day with abundant sunshine and a nice cool breeze. The boys were big now and would be heading off to college in another year. They would soon have lives of their own and where would their lives take them? Shane knew that the boys would never forget the mountains, but depending on what they studied in college, they might remain there or end up with a job in a big city. The boys were taking a walk along the edge of a lake as Shane and Sylvia were sitting on a couple of rocks just talking. "Are you going to miss them when they go off to college?" Sylvia asked.

"Yes, very much but life goes on," he said. "People you love die. Children grow up and have lives of their own, and you never know from one day to the next where your life will lead you."

Sylvia wanted to know how the foundation was going. Shane looked very proud and said, "It is going fine, Sylvia. We have helped so many families. I never imagined that we could do so much for people."

"It is a fine thing you have done, Shane," she told him.

"Sometimes it gets to me when I go talk with someone – in front of a large group of people or when I see a little child who is dying," Shane said. "Then, I realize how much my words have done to help the family and how much aid we have been able to give them financially."

"I'm very proud of you," Sylvia said. "You have done a wonderful thing for many people. I remember the day I saw you on the "Jennifer Wilkins Show." That was one of the most touching and emotional programs I had ever seen in my life."

"I've decided to stay here for a couple of weeks, Shane." She added, "Then, I'm going back to Alabama and put my property up for sale. I will decide during that time where I want to spend the rest of my life."

Shane spoke, "I'm going to hate to see you leave, Sylvia." They looked at each other and smiled. He was thinking, *Should I ask her to stay here? I've been married twice and I've seen two women I love die. I'm scared of being married again.* Sylvia could see his mind was elsewhere. She wondered what was going through his mind. They called the boys and had a nice lunch along the shores of a beautiful lake. Sylvia liked being around the two boys. She often felt badly that she never had any children of her own. They walked back to the car after lunch and Shane drove them back to the inn.

Shane and Sylvia spent a lot of time together during the two weeks that she was there. They often laughed, joked and smiled. They both looked so happy.

One day when Cameron and Shane were alone, Cameron asked, "Do you love her, dad? It's alright if you do. I know mom would want you to be happy."

"I don't know, Cameron, but I know I am very scared of ever being married again." He realized that it was tough to have two special people in his life face tragedy.

"Tyler and I both like Sylvia. She is a very nice woman," Cameron said.

"When did my two boys get so mature and grown up?" Shane said.

Cameron just smiled and added, "When you weren't looking daddy. When you weren't looking."

Sylvia was leaving the inn to go back to Alabama. As he was watching Sylvia walk to the car, he picked up her suitcases and took them to her. Shane said, "Will I ever see you again?"

"I had a wonderful time here, Shane," Sylvia said. "If I ever see you again, it will depend on you." Shane couldn't see it, but Sylvia was crying when she got into the car. She had a torch in her heart for Shane for twenty-five years. She wanted to keep it burning, but how was Shane feeling?

Paul and Peggy were looking out of a window of the inn. Peggy said, "He loves her. I know he does." Knowing it, Paul just nodded.

Chapter Forty

Shane was sitting out in front of his house on the very evening that Sylvia had left. It was one of the few times in his life that he wanted to be left alone. He was staring out into space with a blank look on his face. He didn't know what he should do. He'd been very lonely since Gina passed away. Sure, he had been around many people because of his involvement with the foundation. However, being around people and having someone in your home to talk to – having someone in your bed – were totally different things. He was really feeling that he made a mistake in letting Sylvia go without telling her how much she meant to him.

That very night, Sylvia was sitting in a hotel room somewhere in Pennsylvania. She also felt lonesome – the same way that she had for many years now. She had no doubt in her mind how much she loved Shane. She thought, *Why didn't he stop me? Doesn't he care?* She had no idea how much Shane cared. It was fear that was keeping him from saying anything. She didn't know that. She had a feeling that it was her. Sylvia knew that she was a good person. Now in her fifties, she knew that she didn't want to be alone any longer. She needed someone to hold her and to love her the way she wanted. Two people – one in Vermont and the other in Pennsylvania – were now having strong feelings for each other, after spending two weeks together. Sylvia wondered if she had made a mistake going to

Vermont and telling Shane how she felt. She knew that after reading his book, she had to know.

Cameron walked out of the house and sat in a chair next to Shane. "Dad," he said, "I know you're more afraid than I've ever seen you in my life. You've always been a strong man and would never just sit back and not make a decision that was in your best interest. For some reason, you are holding back. I know you love her. Tell her, dad." Cameron got up and walked back into the house.

Shane knew he was right. What was he doing? Neither one of his wives deaths was his fault. It was life and twice he was given a deal that wasn't fair to him. He had sat in that chair for the longest time, just thinking of Becky and Gina. He loved both of those women so much. Did he have it in him to love another? The last two weeks with Sylvia made him laugh and smile like he hadn't done in years. It was dark when he finally walked into the house. Cameron and Tyler just watched him as he made his way upstairs to the bedroom.

Shane laid in bed for hours without going to sleep. He had been a very fortunate man, even though some of the time was filled with heartache and sorrow. Life has many turns. He kept thinking to himself that there are ups and downs. Many times, when things look down and you feel nothing good will come out of it, you will often be surprised. A perfect example was Gina getting brain cancer. It was one of the lowest periods in his life. However, the upside came when he started the foundation and helped many families going through the emotional and financial troubles that he did. *Sylvia is a fine woman*, he thought. In bed with his eyes wide open, he knew that he had made a mistake in letting her drive away. He sat up on the edge of the bed, looking at the clock. It was now two thirty-six in the morning. *Surely, she would be asleep now,* he thought.

Little did he know that in the Pennsylvania hotel room, Sylvia was going through the same emotional unrest. She stared at the ceiling for hours and was unable to sleep. Was she wrong in letting Shane know how she felt? If she hadn't, he would never know. It was something that she had to do. Sylvia didn't get any sleep until after four o'clock. She was startled when her cell phone rang. "Hello," she answered.

"Sylvia, this is Shane. Did I wake you up? We need to talk," Shane said. He told her how much he cared for her and how afraid he was to love again. He had been married twice and both of them had tragic endings. He told her how he didn't want to be alone anymore.

"I understand, Shane," Sylvia said. "You have had more heartbreak in your life than anyone should have to bear."

Shane asked Sylvia to come back to Vermont. She told him that she had to go home to Alabama first and get her property on the market. "I promise you that I'll come to you after everything is squared away," she said. Shane and Sylvia talked for a few minutes. They both hung up the phone that morning with smiles on their faces.

Shane was going around the Scenic View Inn that morning smiling and singing to himself. Peggy said, "You seem very chipper today, Shane. Do you have something that you would like to share with us?"

"Peggy, I was frightened and scared," he said. "I talked with Sylvia this morning and she will be coming back here after she sells her property in Alabama." Peggy told him that was great news. She could see how much Shane loved Sylvia. Peggy just saw it in his eyes.

Peggy went inside the inn and told Paul about the talk she just had with Shane. "Maybe we'll be having a wedding here soon," said Peggy.

"I think that we will. I really think so," Paul said.

Sylvia called Shane a few weeks after she had her property on the market. She told him that everything seemed to be going fine. "I don't have to stay here, Shane. I can come up there very soon," Sylvia said. Shane told her how much he was looking forward to seeing her again. He wanted Sylvia in his life. It is funny how things go around in a circle. He had met her totally by accident over twenty-five years ago. He had thought of her several times, but apparently, Sylvia thought of him much more than that. He was glad she would be moving to Vermont. He knew that the two of them would get along well. Cameron and Tyler were also glad that she would be coming back. Both of them liked Sylvia very much and the most important thing to them was that their father would be happy again.

Sylvia arrived at the inn just a few weeks later. She didn't need a room in the inn this time. She would be staying in the guest house with Shane. When she arrived, Shane and Sylvia hugged and kissed like they were newly-weds. He said, "I'm so sorry I let you drive away without saying anything to you."

"I understand, Shane," Sylvia said. "You needed some time to think. I did spring my feelings on you very suddenly. I guess I'm the one that should be apologizing."

Shane smiled and said, "Let's take a walk and enjoy the rest of the day." Shane knew that both Becky and Gina were looking down on them smiling. Both of them would always want Shane to be happy. Cameron and Tyler arrived home from school. Both of them hugged Sylvia and welcomed her back. They both loved her and knew she would make Shane a very happy man. Neither one of the boys liked seeing his father so lonesome.

Sylvia got settled in and heard from her realtor in Alabama quite a few times. After a few calls, it sounded like they had someone that was interested in the property. Sylvia owned the house and quite a few acres. It sounded like Sylvia would be able to get around a quarter of a million dollars for the property. It made her happy knowing that she wouldn't have to work for the rest of her life. It was a tough life for her, working in the fields and running the fruit and vegetable stand too. Between what she would receive and what Shane had accumulated from the sale of his book, they would be well off for the rest of their lives. Shane already had the money put away for Cameron's and Tyler's college tuitions. They were still undecided where they wanted to go but would be making a decision soon.

It was about three months after Sylvia arrived back in Vermont that Shane asked her to marry him. Sylvia said, "Yes, oh yes!" Neither of them wanted a big wedding at all. The wedding was in the inn, and except for Paul and Peggy, the only other people in attendance besides Cameron and Tyler were Steve and Sharon Winston.

"I love you, Sylvia," Shane said. She knew he did. It just took him awhile to realize that they were now meant to be with each other. Both of them decided that they didn't want to go on a honeymoon. Being in Vermont with such beautiful mountains all around them was honeymoon enough.

Paul did tell Shane, "You do need to take a week off from work and just enjoy yourselves." Shane was more than happy to do that and he thanked Paul and Peggy for everything they had done for him. He was happy being married again and in the back of his mind, he knew that this one would last forever.

Chapter Forty-One

Shane and Sylvia were a very happy couple. Shane had to admit that he was afraid to get married again, but putting that fear aside was a very wise choice. Sylvia's house in Alabama had been sold and she got a good price. It was strange, in a way, for Sylvia. She had been so used to getting up early and working late all of her life. Being in Vermont, taking nice walks, and enjoying Peggy's company were so nice for her. Sylvia and Peggy often went shopping together. They had to go many miles to get to a larger supermarket. They usually stocked up fairly well, so it turned out to be every other week that they did the shopping.

Cameron and Tyler were spending their first year in college. They both decided to go to a little college outside of Nashville, Tennessee. Shane wondered if it was their love for country music that had an influence on their choice of colleges. It was late in high school when they first learned to play the guitar. Tyler expanded a little and also took up the banjo. Shane and Sylvia both loved the way he picked up the tunes so fast. Both Cameron and Tyler were spending time in Nashville playing at little clubs. It gave them plenty of spending money. Both of them were studying education. Cameron and Tyler both wanted to be teachers. They loved children and they knew that being a teacher would have made their mother proud.

The years ticked by at the Scenic View Inn. Sylvia often helped Peggy make breakfast and dinner for the guests. Sylvia enjoyed doing it. It wasn't a job for her – just something that she wanted to do. Peggy also enjoyed the company and loved having Sylvia's help. Many people were visiting the inn. Quite a few of them brought along a copy of Shane's book and asked him to sign it for them. It seemed strange to Shane to know that people were taking a vacation there just so they could meet him. He continued his work with the foundation. He had talks with families in private and continued to give speeches to high schools and colleges across the northeastern United States. Shane was getting older and he didn't want to make many overnight trips anymore.

So many times, Shane thought of his walk to get to Change, Kansas. He smiled when he thought of that first time that he laid eyes on Gina. It was instantly in Shane's mind that he would ask her to marry him. That was without a doubt the happiest time in his life. He sat out in front of the house one evening. Sylvia peeked out and could see that something was on his mind. She came out and asked, "Ok mister, what is on your mind?"

"I was just thinking. Do you realize in a couple of years I'll be sixty years old?" he said.

"Of course I realize it. I'm not far behind you."

Shane took her hand in his and said, "I love it here, but this isn't our place. It belongs to Paul and Peggy. I want a place of our own." She knew what he meant. He wanted to retire in a couple of years and live out the final days of their lives taking hikes, enjoying the mountain scenery, and fishing.

"We could start looking for a place nearby," she said. "Have you seen that log cabin that is for sale not far from here?"

Shane nodded his head, yes. He liked the looks of that cabin and it had been for sale for quite some time. He knew that it needed some repairs but that was just what he liked to do. In a few days, they got the phone number of the realtor from the sign in the front yard by the cabin. Shane and Sylvia worked out a deal. The cabin was theirs and they knew they would be happy spending the rest of their lives there. Shane gave the news to Paul and Peggy and they weren't surprised at all. Shane said he would be working there for a couple of more years, if it was alright with Paul and Peggy. Paul said, "Of course it is alright. You can work here just as much as you would like to."

"I hope you don't get to be a stranger, Sylvia," Peggy added. "You know how much I like having you around. You have become my best friend."

Sylvia smiled at her and replied, "Don't worry, Peggy. We will remain friends forever." Peggy smiled back at her and gave her a big hug.

Shane and Sylvia spent time working on the cabin. They cleared brush that had grown up around it. The front yard was mowed and soon, it started to look like a real home. When they were finished, they were so proud of the work that they had done. Shane said, "I think that it is time for us to do some relaxing."

Sylvia patted him on the chest, gave him a big hug, and said, "I do too, honey. I love you."

Shane kissed her and said, "I love you too, Sylvia."

Paul and Peggy stopped by to visit and they both said how beautiful the place looked. Shane had bought some rocking chairs and placed them on the front porch. He said, "I got so used to the rockers at the inn that I had to get some." Paul and Peggy smiled. They were so happy for Shane and Sylvia.

"You have had quite a life, haven't you Shane?" Paul said. Shane nodded and told them of how he had left South Carolina to walk west. He had no idea of where he was going and he ended up on a park bench in Change, Kansas where he met Gina. Gina's death was hard on him and the boys. Mainly, because she was in pain for so long. Then, Sylvia, who he had met by accident on his walk so many years ago, came back into his life.

He turned to Sylvia, smiled and said, "Thank you, honey, for making me realize that I could love again. You make me very happy." Sylvia smiled and held Shane's hand with tears running down her cheeks.

They got a phone call that night from Cameron and Tyler. They told Shane that they had met a couple of really nice young women at college. Tyler said, "They both want to be teachers too, Dad." Shane told them that he was glad they were happy and he also said how much they missed both of them.

"We both miss the Vermont mountains, Dad. We think of mom every single day. We loved her so much, but we know that life goes on and are so glad you and Sylvia got married," Cameron said.

Shane thanked them and told them how much he loved them. Shane told them of how they were now settled into their own cabin and how they would now be doing more hiking and fishing. Cameron told Shane that they wouldn't be coming home during the summer. He explained how he, Tyler, and the young women in their lives were renting a two-bedroom apartment on the outskirts of Nashville. Shane was disappointed that they wouldn't be coming home for the summer, but he knew that they were men now and had to lead their own lives.

The years ticked by and it was now the boys' last year in college. In the spring, they would be graduating and getting their degrees. Shane thought back to the day they were born. Shane and Gina had been so happy on that day. He thought, *life sure can change from what you had planned, can't it?* His mind went back to the first time he had ever met Becky. The changes that had taken place since that day were amazing. He was a young man then and now he was into his sixties. He looked at life differently now, knowing that nothing is guaranteed. You can be happy one minute and your life can be shattered the next.

Chapter Forty-Two

It was graduation day at the little college outside of Nashville. As Shane and Sylvia saw Cameron and Tyler receiving their degrees, they knew that their lives would be changing too. Shane was so proud and he knew that Gina was looking down that day with a smile, feeling so proud that they were going to be teachers. Shane had never gone to college and he was happy that the boys could do it.

After the graduation ceremony, Cameron and Tyler brought the two young ladies to meet Shane and Sylvia. Cameron said, "We have some news, Dad. This is Heather and Beth."

Shane and Sylvia told the girls that they were really glad to meet them. Cameron continued, "We're all going to be teaching at a high school very close to here. It's amazing that we all got accepted at the same place. However, the big news is that we're engaged and in about a year, we're having a double wedding ceremony."

Sylvia screeched and said, "That's wonderful news! We're so happy for all of you." Shane and Sylvia hugged the boys and the girls, letting them know how happy they were for them.

When Shane and Sylvia arrived back at the cabin in Vermont, they often thought of Cameron and Tyler. Shane couldn't believe how the boys had matured so much. He always pictured them as little boys, but they were men now. Teachers – what an honorable profession it is. He often smiled as he thought about them. Sylvia sat out front on one of the rocking chairs one day and thought to herself. *Cameron and Tyler are so much like Shane at an early age. They both have the same rugged looks that Shane had when he arrived at my roadside stand so many years ago.* Shane was standing in the doorway and said, "It looks like your mind is a thousand miles away."

She hadn't noticed him standing there. She said, "Yes, I was thinking of how much Cameron and Tyler remind me of you."

Shane and Sylvia were often hiking on the mountain trails. Often times, they would walk past that rock where Shane and Gina had made love on the pile of leaves so many years ago. Shane would always smile when they passed that rock. Sylvia would just look at him, wondering what he was thinking when he got that smile on his face. It was a good thing that she didn't know the whole story. Sylvia was the real outdoors-type and Shane liked that. Their marriage was a happy one and their love for each other kept growing. As they had become older, Shane was working very little at the inn. It gave them more time to spend together and both of them liked that. Paul was kind of sad that Shane was about finished working at the inn, but he knew he needed to settle into retirement.

As one year since graduation was nearing, Shane got a call from Cameron. "Dad, could we have the wedding at the inn?" Shane was so excited and told Cameron that he'd have to ask Paul if it would be alright. Shane immediately called Paul and Paul was more than gracious. Arrangements were made for Heather's and Beth's parents and a few other guests. It was going to be a happy time around the Scenic View Inn. When everyone arrived, they were so pleased with the accommodations and couldn't get over the beauty of the mountains. Shane knew that Cameron, Tyler, Heather, and Beth would be as happy as he had been when he got married.

Having the ceremony at the country inn was beautiful. Heather and Beth loved it there. They didn't want to ever leave. When the reverend pronounced the two happy couples husband and wife and husband and wife, Shane had tears running down his cheeks. They were tears of joy and sorrow at the same time. He was so happy for the boys and their wives and he was so sad that Gina wasn't able to join in on the celebration. After the wedding, there was a great feast in the inn's dining room. Peggy gave them all they could eat. Everyone was so joyous and wished both of the happy couples years of happiness.

Soon, the young newlyweds were on their honeymoons. Cameron and Heather honeymooned in Hawaii and Tyler and Beth went on a cruise to the Caribbean. When the honeymoons came to an end, the happy couples settled into their lives in Nashville. They all lived in the same apartment complex, but Tyler and Beth moved into an apartment of their own. Their first year of teaching went well. It was no doubt that they all made the right decision on what they wanted to do with their lives.

Shane sat on the front porch of the cabin realizing that children grow up and have lives of their own. Also, his were both married now. Shane kept it in his heart that they would always be his little boys. He thought back to the times in Change, Kansas when they were playing ball in the back-yard. He closed his eyes and sat there. *It seems like it was just yesterday,* he thought. How did the years go by so quickly? It had now been fourteen years since Gina died of brain cancer. That was a terrible time in his life. He wished that no family would ever have to go through such a time. He was still getting calls from grieving families. Shane had a way of talking to them how no doctor ever could. His talks came from the heart, because he really did know just how they were feeling.

Sylvia and Shane were happy now. Shane no longer worked at the inn, but they were still good friends with Paul and Peggy. They all had different experiences in their lives. Paul and Peggy had been married a long time. It was now over forty years. Sylvia had lost her husband in a war so far away. It took her years to get over it – even with God's help. Shane had so many ups and downs in his life that he felt like a yo-yo. He had three marriages and loved every one of his wives. Becky was his first love and her car accident shattered Shane's life. God sent him to Gina. He would never forget the times he had with her. He still thought of the time when she asked him to hug her and she died in his arms. At the time, it seemed like the end of the world. It was years later that he reconnected with a woman he had met some twenty-five years earlier. Sylvia was a wonderful, sweet, and kind woman. He was afraid of asking her to marry him. Shane was so worried that if they married, God would take her from him. They had been happily married for many years now. They were happy years of a life together in the mountains of Vermont.

Shane used to be fearful of talking with families about someone who was terminally ill. He got over that fear many years ago and had done so much to help families. In the past year, he had given over ten speeches to colleges in the New England area. College students were amazed at how Shane expressed himself. Often times, they would bring a copy of his book up to him after a speech and asked if he would sign it for them. Many of them would tell him of a death in their family and how reading his book made the grieving process easier. Gina's death somehow had brought peace to many families. Shane would often look at the sky and say, "We have helped many people, Gina."

Chapter Forty-Three

It wasn't many years later when Shane got word that he was going to be a grandfather. Sylvia might have been Cameron and Tyler's stepmother, but in their eyes, she would be their kids' grandmother. They were so happy that she made their father like a whole man again. Heather and Beth each had children. Shane and Sylvia had to take a trip to Nashville to see them. Shane was in his sixties and seeing those little children made him feel young again. Heather had a boy and Beth had a girl. Just watching Shane and Sylvia brought smiles to the faces of Cameron and Tyler.

The boys and their wives continued to live in Nashville. Their teaching careers were going very well. Teaching made all of them feel proud of what they were doing. Shane and Sylvia retired to the mountains of Vermont. Sitting on the front porch in their rocking chairs and watching the sun set over the mountains was something they liked to do every night – at least, until the weather turned too cold for them to sit outside. Snow came early to the mountains and made it a true winter wonderland. Shane spent much time clearing snow from the driveway and sidewalk to the cabin. It was still a great life spending time in the outdoors.

Sylvia did much baking and prepared fine meals. They often took Shane back to the time she made him meals in her home in Alabama. Shane said, "Do you miss Alabama, Sylvia?"

"Yes, sometimes I do," she said. "I guess your mind always goes to where you were born and raised." They knew it was a different time in their lives now. They were getting old but still young enough to enjoy life. They couldn't think of any place they would rather spend their final years.

It was a cold and cloudy day when Sylvia decided to take the long drive to buy food. Peggy couldn't go along with her for some reason. Sylvia got to the store fine and did her shopping so she could have a good two week supply of food. It seemed like a nice day, but it was starting to snow heavily as she pulled out of the store parking lot. She was driving slowly, but as she rounded one of the mountain curves, a herd of deer was standing right in the road. She slammed on the brakes and the car went into a spin, sliding off the edge of the road and down a steep hill. The car went out of control and hit a tree, which stopped it from going into a creek. The snow was falling very heavily and would soon cover the area where she went off the highway.

Sylvia was knocked unconscious for a short time. She woke up shivering and knew she had to get out of the car. It was no use. Her right leg was pinned under the dash. Sylvia started to cry. She knew if Shane or someone else didn't find her soon, it was going to be a cold time waiting. Sylvia always kept blankets in the car in case something like this might happen. She could barely reach into the back seat and pull them up to her. She covered up and felt warm. Shane was getting concerned when it was getting near dark and Sylvia still hadn't come home. He called the state police and reported her missing. They told Shane that they would do what they could, but the weather was getting very bad.

It was well past midnight and Sylvia still hadn't made it home. The state police had driven by where Sylvia had gone off the road, but they couldn't see the spot because of the snow. They called Shane and said they had driven the highway and saw no sign of her car. Shane sat down and started to cry. This couldn't be happening again. *Where is she?* he thought. Shane paced inside the cabin all night. Sylvia was awake all night. She knew she couldn't doze off. Shane had prayed for Gina and now he was praying for Sylvia. *She can't be dead,* he thought. Shane got down on his knees and prayed to God. "Please, bring back Sylvia to me, God. Where is she? Is she hurt? Is she alright? I have to know. I need your help," he said. Tears were streaming down Shane's face. He had been so happy and now – another tragedy.

It was early morning and Sylvia did close her eyes for a few minutes. She woke up cold, sore, and wondering if Shane was looking for her. She looked out her window and saw that the snow was so deep. Turning her head to the right, she saw an angel sitting next to her. Sylvia asked, "Oh my God, am I going to die?"

The angel had a glow to her and said, "Hang on, Sylvia. Don't give up hope. You will be found."

"I feel so cold," Sylvia said. The entire car was glowing and was getting warmer.

The angel said to her, "You are going to be alright. Shane will come for you."

Sylvia leaned her head back to rest and when she again looked to the right, the angel was gone. *Am I hallucinating?* she thought. No, she wasn't. She was still warm. The car was still glowing. It was warm.

It was just a little before daybreak and Shane was sitting close to the fire. He lifted up his head and saw God sitting in the chair next to him. God said, "Sylvia is alive, Shane. She has been in an accident. I have sent an angel to her. It is up to you to find her. The snow is too deep, so you will have to walk."

"How will I find her?" Shane asked.

"Follow the light, Shane. I will guide you to her." Shane put on his snow shoes and walked out of the cabin. The snow was so deep. He had to find her. He just had to. He looked to the sky and saw the light. He walked toward it, following the road. Walking was hard because of the snow. God was right. The light kept him moving. It was three hours later when the light started to flash. It was right above him. Was he here? Was Sylvia here? He couldn't see her. He turned his head and could see that something had run through the brush.

It had to be her. He knew it, as he struggled to get down the hill safely. Soon, he could see the car. He got the door open and Sylvia turned to him and smiled. She said, "I knew you were coming. The angel told me you would come."

Shane put his arms around her and held her tight. She was alive. He was so afraid all night. He walked again in his life to the one he loved. The car still glowed with warmth. Shane couldn't get Sylvia's leg free from under the dash. He knew he had to get help but couldn't get a signal on his cell phone. He again made it to the top of the hill where he could get a signal, called the state police and told them of his location. Shane said, "She is pinned in the car. She'll need an ambulance." The state police knew an ambulance couldn't get through. The snow had stopped. They told Shane they would be there soon and were going to send a helicopter to take her to the hospital. They told him to stay on the road so they could find him easier.

Sylvia was freed from the car. As she was being freed, the rescuers looked at the car that was still glowing and felt warm. Sylvia looked at them and said, "An angel came to me. She kept me warm." The rescuers looked at her and smiled. They got her up the hill and into the helicopter. Shane thanked the state police and got into the helicopter to ride with her. They were on the way to the hospital. Sylvia was going to be fine. She was saved with the help of God.

During the flight, she kept repeating, "Thank you, God. Thank you, God." Shane was tired beyond belief, but kept smiling at Sylvia. His wife this time wasn't leaving him to go to heaven. She had much more time to look forward to on earth.

Chapter Forty-Four

Shane was sitting in the waiting room at the hospital emergency room as the doctors were attending to Sylvia. He couldn't sit still. He just paced back and forth in the room. It was soon when one of the nurses came out to him and gave him an update. She told him that Sylvia looked as good as could be expected for what she had gone through. Her leg was broken and she had several cracked ribs, many cuts and bruises; however, she would be fine. Sylvia would have to stay in the hospital for a day or two, but soon would be back with Shane.

Shane soon was allowed in to see Sylvia. She said, "I knew you would find me, Shane. The angel told me that you would."

"God came to me, Sylvia," replied Shane. "He told me to follow the light. It took me some hard walking through the snow, but He led me to you. How are you feeling?"

Sylvia told him that it would be awhile. She was sore, but she was alive. She said, "I was so scared when it happened. I thought I was going to freeze to death. When I saw the angel next to me, I knew it was going to be alright. She saved me, Shane. She kept the car warm. If it wasn't for her, I would have frozen to death." Shane told her it was surely a walk to love that brought him to her.

It was two days later when Sylvia arrived back at the cabin. She had a cast on her leg and her ribs were taped up. She was sore – so very sore – but she was home. The cabin never looked so good to her. Shane waited on her hand and foot. She said, "You are going to spoil me, honey."

"I love you so much, honey," he said. "I was so scared when you didn't come home and it was snowing so hard. I kept thinking that I couldn't possibly have another wife die. I cried and I cried wondering what had happened to you." Sylvia told him of the deer in the road.

It took a long time for Sylvia to get around again. She spent much time sitting in a chair in front of the fire. She always loved the fireplace. It looked so peaceful to her. Peggy visited her often and they would sit there together and talk about old times. Peggy said, "When Shane called me and asked if you were at the inn, I was so scared. It was snowing so hard and we both feared the worst. I never prayed so much in my life. Thank God he found you."

"I never saw snow like that in Alabama. I guess I never should have decided to go to the store that day. It didn't look bad when I left," Sylvia said.

Cameron and Tyler often called from Nashville and asked how Sylvia was doing. She so much enjoyed their phone calls. Sylvia was so happy about the way the boys accepted her into the family. She knew in her heart that those calls helped her get better. The soreness was going away and Sylvia was able to get around with crutches. She just couldn't wait until the day the cast finally came off of her leg. The day finally did come and life was starting to get back to normal. She was back to her old self again. It was a wonderful feeling. Shane and Sylvia often thanked God. *God really does listen,* she thought to herself so many times. Shane came home one evening after helping Paul with something at the inn and saw Sylvia crying. "What's wrong, honey? What's wrong?" he asked.

"Nothing, sweetheart. Nothing. I'm just so happy. These are happy tears you are looking at. I love you, Shane

Donaldson." He hugged and kissed her and told her how much he loved her.

It was another bad time in Shane's life, but thankfully, this one had a happy ending. Although there were many ups and downs in Shane's life, he was a happy man. Spring finally came to Vermont. The birds were chirping, the days were getting warmer, and the bare trees were getting leaves again. Autumn was always Shane's favorite time of the year, but springtime was a close second. He sat on the front porch knowing that this was where he wanted to spend his final years. He was in his upper sixties now, but got around like a man much younger. Hikes in the mountains were what he wanted to do. He often hiked with Sylvia, but there were times when he wanted to go alone. Sylvia never questioned why. She knew that he needed some time to be alone with his thoughts. On several occasions, he hiked to the rock where he and Gina had made love so many years ago.

He talked to her like she was going to answer him back. Shane knew she was in heaven looking down on him. Gina never would have wanted him to be sad. Shane got up from the tree he was leaning against and made a pile of leaves behind the rock. Finishing, he sat back down, leaning against the tree once again. He smiled and looked up to the heavens. He said, "Gina, do you remember that day here?" Shane was thinking back to so many good times in his life. Becky, Gina, and now Sylvia had shown him more love than any man deserved. To find love three times in one's life was truly an honor that few men would ever be able to share. It was getting late in the afternoon on that day. Shane looked up in the sky and saw a cloud with an unusual formation. It was moving into a clump, forming a person's face. He kept staring as it formed. A smile broke out on his face. It was Gina. That cloud was Gina. She was staring down on him with a smile on her face. He smiled and said, "I will always love you, Gina." The cloud moved apart and Shane sat there knowing that Gina had heard him. *She really heard me,* he thought. Walking back to the car, he couldn't get out of his mind what had just happened.

He walked into the cabin late that afternoon with a smile on his face. Sylvia was sitting in a chair reading a book when he arrived home. She said, "Did you have a good day, honey?"

He smiled at her and said, "Yes, it was a very good day." Shane wanted to know what she had been doing while he was gone. She told him that she went to the inn awhile and talked with Peggy and then came home and started to do some reading. Shane wanted to know how Paul and Peggy were doing. Sylvia told him that they just loved the inn. Shane knew that they did. When they moved from Atlanta to buy that inn in Vermont, it changed their lives in a way that many people couldn't understand. Paul often told Shane that money is nice, but happiness is a whole lot more rewarding. It took Shane some time to realize what Paul had meant, but when he looked at those mountains, he knew exactly. Sylvia and Shane were a happy couple and knowing that they would probably stay here until the day they died was always on their minds.

Chapter Forty-Five

Sylvia was walking with a slight limp, but that was something she would have to deal with for the rest of her life. As she always said, "It is just a minor inconvenience." She often thought back to the accident and knew there really were angels. Shane often wondered why God decided to save Sylvia but not save Gina. He was thankful for every one of his marriages. However, if he had to pick the one that meant the most to him, he would have to pick Gina. Maybe it was walking halfway across the country to meet her. Maybe it was just that they both had tragic events in their lives. He loved Sylvia very much and that would continue forever.

Sylvia never went to the store again by herself – even in the summertime. She knew she could have done it, but the accident really put a fear into her that she couldn't explain. Sylvia and Peggy made those trips every other week. It was good for both of them. It gave them some time to talk about their lives and to share some things about Shane and Paul. Sylvia was pushing seventy now and Shane was already in his early seventies. They were both in good shape and continued to lead the lives that they wanted to. Shane and Sylvia continued to take a nice hike in the mountains a couple of times a week. One weekend, Sylvia asked Peggy if she and Paul would like to join them.

"Oh yes, we would. Paul will have to get someone to watch the inn for us," Peggy said.

It was the following weekend when the four of them took a nice trail that Shane was unaware of. Paul had known about this trail for years, but he didn't tell many people. They hiked in about three miles from where they parked their car. Around the last bend in the trail, a large lake appeared in front of them. Shane said, "This is beautiful, Paul! You've been holding out on me."

Paul just laughed and said, "I'm glad you like it." They fished for most of the morning. The lake was just teeming with large fish. They decided to keep a few and released most of them back into the cold water of the lake. Paul built a little campfire and pulled a frying pan out of his backpack. He knew they would be catching some fish and wanted to fry them right away. He was the master of the frying pan that day and placed the fish and beans onto the paper plates that Peggy had in her backpack. It was so delicious. Everything seemed so much better when made over a campfire.

"Do you like blueberries, Sylvia?" Peggy asked.

"Oh yes, I love them."

"Well, what do you say we go pick some while the men just hang around and enjoy the lake?" suggested Peggy. They walked a few hundred yards into the forest and came to a clearing that was covered with blueberry bushes. They talked and picked and ate way too many of them as they were doing so. Peggy said, "I think I'll bake a blueberry pie tonight."

"I'm sure Shane would enjoy having one too," Sylvia said. It was a few hours later when they arrived back by the lake and saw both Paul and Shane fast asleep under the shade of the large trees. Peggy and Sylvia just sat down and talked for the longest time. Shane was first to wake up and Sylvia said, "It's about time, sleepyhead."

Peggy just laughed and said, "Look at my ambitious man over there. He looks dead to the world." Shane told

Peggy and Sylvia that there was no doubt they were all getting older.

Paul continued to sleep for over an hour more, often snoring loudly. Shane said, "Do you put up with that every night?"

Peggy just nodded her head and smiled. "There is no one I would rather listen to that sounds like a buzz saw," she said. They were all laughing but they realized they were all in their very late sixties to late seventies. They were on the downhill side of life and were going to take advantage of every second that they could.

Paul finally woke up, looked at everyone staring at him, and said, "How long have I been asleep?"

"All night, sweetie. Do you realize it is now Sunday?" Peggy said. Paul got a blank look on his face, until everyone started to laugh so hysterically. Paul thought for a minute that Peggy was serious.

He stuck his tongue out at her and said, "Very funny. I really thought I had."

Paul said to Shane, "What do you say we catch a few more fish to take home with us?" Shane thought it was a great idea. They picked up their fishing poles, while Peggy and Sylvia decided to stay where they were and take their turn at resting and talking for a while. Sylvia and Peggy just looked out over the lake and commented on how beautiful it looked. Peggy said, "I never want to go back to the city. I belong here. Paul and I have been here a long time and this is where I want to die."

"Don't talk about dying. You have many years of life yet," Sylvia said. Peggy was sure she did, but it was a fact that they were all growing older. Every one of them had gray hair now. That was something that Peggy had to point out. Sylvia said, "I was a young woman when I first met Shane. I kept him in my heart for years, hoping that someday we would meet again. Isn't it funny how things work out?" Peggy agreed that many strange things happen in a person's life that can't be explained.

A couple of hours later, the men arrived back carrying some nice fish. The men enjoyed the fishing just as much as the women enjoyed picking the blueberries. They cleaned up around the site, put their backpacks on, and started walking back to the car, carrying the fish and berries. When they got back home, they were tired but had such a wonderful day that they decided to do it every once in a while.

When Shane checked his email that evening, he saw that he had photos from Tyler. Everyone looked so nice and Tyler's daughter was growing so fast. Shane missed them. He thought of the boys every day. They have had good lives. He was so glad that Cameron and Tyler met two women that they loved so much. All of their teaching careers were going well. Sylvia walked into the room and he showed the photos to her. She smiled and said, "You really love your boys, don't you?"

He smiled and nodded his head as he pulled Sylvia close to him. He ran his hands through her hair and said, "Thank you, Sylvia, for giving me so much love."

At the bottom of the email, Tyler wrote that he wanted to come back to the mountains for Thanksgiving – actually, everyone wanted to come. Shane immediately wrote back and said that he loved the idea. Arrangements were made at the inn to put up the boys and their families. Shane would have liked having them at the cabin, but it was just too small for everyone. Shane counted off the days for a few months until Thanksgiving finally arrived.

Chapter Forty-Six

The day before Thanksgiving, Cameron, Tyler, and their families arrived at the inn. They got settled into their rooms and immediately went to see Shane and Sylvia at their cabin. They all loved the cabin. It looked so cozy. The views were fantastic. Tyler said, "This is even more beautiful for real than it was in the photos that you sent us." They all agreed. It was beautiful and having everyone together for Thanksgiving was a dream.

On Thanksgiving, Sylvia joined Heather and Beth at the inn early. Peggy had told them they would have Thanksgiving dinner there. It was early when they started to prepare the feast that they would have that afternoon. The women all talking together in the kitchen was the most enjoyable time of the day for them. Peggy loved having everyone there. It had been a long time since she had so many people around on Thanksgiving. Beth said, "What are you all thankful for?" Each of the women looked at each other and started to think.

Peggy went first. She said, "I'm thankful that Paul and I moved here years ago and bought this inn nestled in the beautiful mountains of Vermont."

Sylvia had tears in her eyes as she said, "It was years and years ago when I first met Shane. He never left my mind. When I read his book, I knew that I had to see him again. I'm so thankful that he asked me to marry him."

Heather took her turn saying, "Graduating from college had been a wonderful time in my life. Also, meeting Cameron and becoming his wife has made me thankful every day."

Beth started the conversation, but she wanted to go last. Her words were, "I have so much to be thankful for, but I think today is ranked number one for me. I'm thankful that for the first time in our lives we are all together." Every one of the women hugged each other with tears in their eyes. It seemed that Beth's words touched them the most. Little did they know that this Thanksgiving was the last time they would all be together!

In the mid-afternoon, they all gathered in the dining room of the inn. It was quite a group of family and friends. Four guests also joined them for the Thanksgiving feast. One of them, a man from Florida, asked if he could say the blessing. It was so nice and made everyone fill with happiness. Turkey, ham, stuffing, cranberry sauce, potatoes, green beans, carrots, sweet rolls and drinks filled the table of the inn that day. All of them ate so much that they were stuffed. They all kind of felt like they were turkeys themselves. The dinner was topped off with a piece of pumpkin pie with a scoop of ice cream on top.

Shane wasn't saying much but he was looking around at how happy everyone looked. He stood up and wanted to say a few words, "I'm so happy and proud that everyone is here today. Also, thanks to our guests from other states. In all the years I have lived, which is now well into the seventies, I have to say without a doubt that this is the best Thanksgiving Day I have ever had. I want to thank my sons, their wives, their children, and Paul and Peggy for making this a memorable day for me. I would like to end by saying, Sylvia, I love you. You have made me a very happy man for many years."

Everyone had tears running down their cheeks. Shane's words were so inspiring. Cameron and Tyler hugged their father. They loved him so much and thanked him for everything he had done for them. They knew that Shane always supported them in everything they had done all their lives. Shane never pushed them to do anything. He talked to them and guided them, but the final decision on what they wanted to do was always up to them. Cameron and Tyler hugged Sylvia and both of them whispered in her ear, "I love you, Sylvia. Thank you for making dad so happy." She couldn't control her emotions. She hugged and hugged the boys – not wanting to let go of them. They didn't realize how much their words meant to her.

It was Sunday around noon when the boys and their families started on their journey back to Nashville. They didn't want to leave, but they knew school started on Tuesday and they wanted to get some rest before they went in to teach. Shane and Sylvia spent some time with the grandchildren on that last morning before they left. Shane watched them drive away. It seemed so hard on him – watching them go down the driveway and disappear out of sight.

It was several days before Shane said much. He loved having Sylvia around and hugged her as they sat on the sofa, but his words were few and far between. Sylvia said, "Is something wrong, Shane?"

He smiled at her and said, "No, not really. I was just wondering if I will ever see my boys again. I'm getting old, Sylvia. How many more years do I have? And, the boys have their own lives. They love it in Nashville and I'm glad they are doing well. I just wonder if I will ever see their faces again." Sylvia knew and understood what Shane was saying. Yes, they were getting older. She was thinking of how Paul and Peggy looked so old. She didn't think that they would be able to keep the inn running much longer by themselves. She felt that she and Shane were so lucky that they had enough money to live the rest of their lives without working.

Shane got a call from Cameron saying that they had arrived back in Nashville safely. He said, "I love you, Dad. We all had a wonderful time seeing you again." Shane felt empty as he hung up the phone. It had been a wonderful Thanksgiving, but he had a strange feeling that it would be the last time he spent it with the boys. *Boys,* he thought, *they aren't boys. They are grown men that I am proud of.*

Shane snuggled under the covers that night after giving Sylvia a kiss and saying, "Good night, honey. I love you so much." She smiled and told him that she loved him too.

It was getting colder in the Vermont Mountains as Christmas approached. From the looks of it, they were going to have a white Christmas. It did start snowing early on the morning of Christmas Eve and continued until almost dark on Christmas Day. Shane had plenty of firewood inside the cabin. He told Sylvia that they would be as snug as a bug in a rug. She laughed and said, "You always say the funniest things." They spent much time on Christmas sitting in chairs in front of the fire just talking about their lives. They both came from the south, so a white Christmas was something they never saw until they moved to Vermont.

"There is just something about snow on Christmas that makes it seem so real," Shane said. Sylvia knew what he meant. It was a totally different experience spending Christmas where it was warm in the south. She looked out the window several times to see the snow falling. It looked so beautiful sticking to the trees.

It was late on Christmas Day when Cameron and Tyler called them from Nashville. Cameron said, "I see by the weather that it is snowing there."

Shane told him how beautiful it was. Tyler wanted to know what they were doing. Sylvia told them that they were sitting in front of the fire drinking a mug of hot chocolate.

Tyler said, "That sounds like a wonderful way to spend Christmas."

They were all on speaker phone at Cameron's apartment. Heather said, "We have something for you guys. We hope you like it." It was silent for a second and then they heard Cameron, Tyler, Heather, and Beth singing "Jingle Bells," followed by "Silent Night." Shane and Sylvia were laughing as they clapped and told them how much they appreciated it.

When they hung up the phones, Shane said, "They weren't here, but it was a nice Christmas present they gave us. I love them all." Sylvia said that she did too. They finished their hot chocolate and then watched some television until it was time to go to bed. They laid down with visions of sugar plums dancing in their heads. It was a wonderful day.

Chapter Forty-Seven

For New Year's Eve, Paul and Peggy invited Shane and Sylvia to spend it with them at the inn. They were having several couples staying there the week between Christmas and New Year's. A party was planned with a nice buffet and dancing throughout the night. Shane and Sylvia were so glad they were invited. It had been quite a while since they danced together. Walking into the inn, they saw quite a few people mingling about. Shane and Sylvia walked around introducing themselves to all of the couples. The ages varied from a young couple in their early twenties up to an old couple that was about their age.

The old man said, "Hey, aren't you Shane Donaldson? You didn't give your last name but I thought it was you. Our daughter developed brain cancer about ten years ago. Shane, if it wasn't for your book, I don't think my wife and I would have ever been able to get through the ordeal. After reading your book, we realized with her in a coma for a week, it just wasn't the same woman we raised. We took her off of life support and let God take her. We know she went to a better place." Shane and Sylvia said how sorry they were. They knew it was tough loosing someone you love so much.

They all went through the buffet line and filled up their plates. Sylvia said, "You should have called me, Peggy. I would have given you a hand preparing this lovely meal."

Peggy told her that she thought about it but didn't want to bother her during the holidays. The two women hugged and sat down alone at a corner table where they talked for the longest time. Music was playing and Paul walked over to Peggy and said, "May I have this dance, my love?"

Peggy smiled, then got up and went to dance with Paul. Shane came over and sat next to Sylvia. He said, "They really are a nice couple, aren't they? They have been married close to sixty years. That is a long time."

"Yes it is, but I think running the inn is getting to be too hard on them," Sylvia said.

"I know. I was just talking to Paul," Shane replied. "He told me it was and that in the spring they are putting the inn up for sale."

"Are they going to stay around here?" Sylvia asked. Shane just shrugged his shoulders. He didn't know.

It was just about midnight when the music was turned off and the television was turned on. They were looking at Times Square in New York City. It was a New Year's tradition that they watched the ball drop. The ball started to move and everyone counted down the seconds. It was a New Year and all of the couples kissed each other. Shane and Sylvia sat down with Paul and Peggy and reminisced about all of the fun they had at the inn. They had spent many years together. Shane was thinking ... it had been a long time since he and Gina had come to the inn years and years ago to look at the autumn colors. He was smiling. Sylvia just glanced at him knowing that his mind was elsewhere. "You are in a different time in your life," she said.

"I didn't know that I was that obvious," he said.

Sylvia replied, "That's all right, honey. I understand. I really do." Shane had been a lucky man in his life in so many ways. He looked at Sylvia and realized spending his last years on earth with her had brought him so much happiness.

The rest of the winter brought some nasty weather, but an early spring did arrive. Shane was visiting Paul one day when he saw a "FOR SALE" sign on the front yard of the inn. Paul walked outside and came up to Shane.

"I see you are really going through with it," Shane said.

"Yes, I have mixed feelings," Paul said. "It's just hard for Peggy and I to hang on to it any longer. We're in our eighties, Shane. We need a few years to relax. When we sell, we are going to move to Florida." Shane and Sylvia would hate to see them go, but he knew they needed some time to enjoy life. Shane told Paul to please let them know before they left.

Shane was sitting out on the front porch that night just looking at the stars. Sylvia was watching him out the window and knew he was thinking about something serious. Whenever he had something serious on his mind, he would do that. Sylvia was thinking about how much she would miss Peggy. Peggy had been her best friend for a long time. They often talked about things that they wouldn't tell anyone else. She went out to the porch and sat in a rocking chair next to Shane. "Are you going to tell me what is on your mind, old man?"

He just smiled and said, "We're getting very old too, Sylvia. Do you think it is smart for us to live in the cold, snowy north any longer?" She wanted to know if he was considering moving to Florida. Shane nodded his head and told her that maybe it was a smart thing to do.

"We've known Paul and Peggy for a long time," she said. "I know I would miss them something fierce." Shane just kept staring straight ahead. Sylvia could tell he was seriously thinking about moving to Florida. She could see it by his actions.

Finally, Shane said, "Let's move to Florida and live next to Paul and Peggy."

"Great idea. Let's go tell them now," Sylvia said. They drove to the inn, walked inside and told Paul and Peggy what they wanted to do. Everyone was hugging.

"We were thinking of moving a couple of years ago but didn't want to leave you guys. After all, you are our best friends," Paul said.

"We're thinking of living somewhere along the gulf coast. What do you think?" Peggy said. Shane and Sylvia told them that it was a great idea.

The inn was sold in the summer. Paul hoped the new owners would like it as much as he and Peggy did for so many years. Shane told Sylvia that he wanted to give the cabin to the boys. They could come up to the cabin any time they wanted to get away from the rat race. Sylvia loved the boys and she knew that they would like to have it. The four of them were heading to Florida – going to unchartered territory, as Shane would say. They ended up buying apartments in a condominium on the gulf coast. It was such a change for them, but they knew that they had made the right choice. Life was so relaxing, in what all of them knew was their final years. The four of them were into their early to late eighties, but all were in good health. Paul and Shane took up golf. Neither one of them were very good, especially at the start. However, with some practice, they didn't look too bad and enjoyed getting out on the course a couple of mornings a week.

Sylvia and Peggy joined a senior women's club that was organized by the condominium. They often took day trips around to different attractions of interest. The weather was what they enjoyed the most. It was always so warm. Sylvia said, "Just think, Peggy, no more snow to deal with."

Peggy smiled, knowing that she would miss the mountains, especially around Christmas time. Peggy had a hidden fear of dying that none of the others knew about. It was a fear that ran deep into her soul. Often at night, she would lay in bed thinking to herself: *I hope I die first. I don't want to live if Paul isn't with me.* They were sitting outside on some lawn chairs when Sylvia could see that something was on her mind. She didn't want to pry. Just as well, she wouldn't have known what to say anyway. When people get old, they know that the day is coming when they will take their last breath.

It was a little over a year later when Peggy died. Paul was devastated. He loved Peggy so much – from the first time he ever laid eyes on her. She was buried in a cemetery not far from the condo. Paul made daily trips to visit at her grave with tears in his eyes. He often brought flowers. He said, "I know how much you like flowers, honey." He laid them next to the grave marker. He often thought to himself: *Maybe, we should have moved here sooner. I know working at the inn was hard on you, especially in the winter.*

Shane and Sylvia often talked about how Paul hadn't been the same since Peggy died. Paul never went to play golf again. He would say he was just too old, however, Shane knew better. Sitting in their living room one night, Shane said, "I wonder which one of us will be next."

"It better not be you, Mr. Donaldson," Sylvia said. "I need you." He smiled at her and gave her a hug.

It was a long time before Shane went to bed that night. The television was turned on, but he wasn't looking at it. Sylvia had gone to bed earlier. Shane just sat there and thought about his life. He looked at it from every angle. There were good times. There were bad times. Sitting there one minute, he would have a huge smile on his face and the next minute, tears would be streaming down his cheeks. He was tired and getting more and more tired every day. He missed Paul. Every time he went to see him, Paul just sat there – not looking at TV, not reading, just sitting there like life had no meaning. Peggy's death had really taken a toll on him. Life didn't seem to have a purpose anymore. Shane still had Sylvia, but Paul had no one. He had no idea that living alone would be so hard.

Shane would go home to Sylvia and say, "He doesn't want to talk or do anything. He just sits there and stares straight ahead. He doesn't look good, Sylvia. I'm worried about him, but I don't know what to do." Sylvia held Shane's hand. She didn't know what to do either. It was hard seeing someone you love just give up on life.

Chapter Forty-Eight

Shane and Sylvia were seeing less and less of Paul. It was approaching the holiday season and they wanted to do something to get Paul back and feeling alive again. The day before Thanksgiving, Shane called Paul's apartment numerous times. He didn't answer and Shane was becoming increasingly worried. Shane decided to go and pound on his door. In the back of his mind, he felt that something was wrong. *Maybe he had fallen down and just couldn't make it to the phone,* he thought. Paul didn't answer the door and Shane couldn't hear any sounds coming from inside.

Shane got the building manager. They opened the door and saw Paul lying on the floor with a plastic bag over his head. Shane was so shocked. He couldn't believe his eyes. Lying on the floor next to Paul was a note. Shane picked it up and Shane and the building manager looked at it. It said that he didn't want to live anymore and that he wanted to be with Peggy. Paul had committed suicide. Never in a million years would Shane have thought that Paul would do such a thing. The building manager called the police and told them what had happened. When the police arrived, they asked Shane questions about Paul. Shane filled them in about his wife dying and that he had been severely depressed ever since her death.

After the body was removed from the apartment, Shane walked back to his, which was on one floor lower. He walked in and immediately Sylvia knew that something was wrong. She said, "What is it Shane? What's wrong?"

Shane just sat down and shook his head. "I can't believe it, honey. I just can't believe it," he said. He looked up at Sylvia and said, "He's dead. He committed suicide. He left a note saying that he wanted to go and be with Peggy."

Sylvia sat down beside Shane and put her arms around him. "I'm so sorry. I'm so terribly sorry," she said. Shane had known them for so many years and couldn't believe that two of the best friends that he ever had in his life were gone. They both had been so good to Shane ever since he first met them in Vermont.

"He should have moved south sooner. Running the inn in his later years just took so much out of him," Shane said. Sylvia knew it had taken a toll on both Peggy and Paul; however, each of them loved the mountains. It was their home. They couldn't imagine living anywhere else for years.

Paul was buried next to Peggy. His death was harder on Shane than it was on Sylvia. Sylvia could see that Shane was trying to put on a good front, but she could see the hurt in his eyes. Shane said to her one day, "If he had just died, it wouldn't have bothered me so much, but he killed himself." Sylvia knew that Shane had seen more death in his life than anyone should have to. With the foundation, he would visit families and give them good advice and tell them what they should expect. Paul was his best friend. He saw that something was wrong. Why couldn't he say something? Why couldn't he find the right words to say to him? He always knew what to say to perfect strangers, but not to someone that he cared for so deeply.

It worried Shane for a long time; however, he had to move forward and not dwell on the past. He often talked with Cameron and Tyler. They had used the cabin in Vermont several times. They told Shane how much they appreciated being able to use it and get some peace and quiet for a while. Shane learned that the new people running the Scenic View Inn were doing well. It took Shane's mind back to the first day that Gina and he saw it for the first time. He had no idea at that time that he would be living there. Every time he thought of the place, he had to think of when he made love on the pile of leaves with Gina. He knew that someday his ashes would be spread there with Gina's. *That is the way it is meant to be,* he thought to himself.

Shane had much in his life to be thankful for. He tried to think more of those times and less about the times that broke his heart. He knew that everyone had challenges that they have to face. No matter what age you are or where you live, there are always things that come at you unexpectedly. Shane was so thankful that he had God in his life. If it wasn't for God, he might have died a young man in South Carolina. Wow, that was so many years ago! He would never forget the walk halfway across America that changed his life. Shane often thought of the women in his life. They were the ones that made him realize that life is worth living. Thinking of each of them brought a smile to his face – Becky, Gina, and now Sylvia. He really was a very lucky man.

Shane often took his thoughts back to the Thanksgiving when all of the family had celebrated with Paul and Peggy and some other hotel guests. He had the feeling then that it would be the last time they were all together on Thanksgiving. It was one of the greatest Thanksgivings he ever had in his life. This Thanksgiving was far from happy. He couldn't get his mind off of Paul. They had so many good times together. Shane would often sit out on the balcony and feel so sad that Paul was gone. He knew that in time, the hurt would heal and the good memories would come back to him. Paul and Peggy were two of the nicest people that he had ever met in his life. They had a perfect marriage. In all the time he had known them, he never once heard a cross word between them.

Sylvia came out and sat on the balcony with Shane. Sylvia said, "You keep thinking a lot of Paul, don't you?" Shane just nodded his head. She said, "I miss Peggy too. I wish so much that the two of them were here with us right now. That is life, Shane. People that you love die and there isn't anything in the world that we can do to stop it." Shane knew that she was right, but for now, the pain didn't want to go away.

Christmas was approaching for another year and the good news was that the boys and their wives were coming to Florida to spend it with Shane and Sylvia. When they arrived, it was a happy time. It was the first time they had seen the condo and all were impressed with how nice it was. It was Tyler that broke the news to them. Tyler said, "Dad, we know you are really getting up there in years. We want to spend some time with you and Sylvia. We're all planning on moving to Florida in the spring, so we can be close to the two of you." Shane was so happy. He couldn't believe what he was hearing. They were all applying for teaching jobs in the area around where Shane lived.

In the spring, the boys and their wives arrived just like they had promised. They knew that Heather and Beth would love the Florida sunshine. It didn't take much convincing from Cameron and Tyler for them to agree to the move. They all got teaching jobs, but not in the same school like they were able to do around Nashville. However, none of them had to drive very far. It was a dream come true for Shane, and Sylvia could see that he was happy – very happy again. When tragedy struck like it did with the deaths of Paul and Peggy, it took family to make life look bright again.

Shane pulled Cameron aside one day and said, "Remember when I spread mom's ashes near that rock in Vermont? I asked you at that time to do the same with my ashes. You didn't forget, did you?"

"No, Dad. I didn't forget," Cameron said. "I know how much you loved mom and when the time comes, Tyler and I will see to it that we grant you that wish."

Shane hugged Cameron and just said, "Thank you, son." Cameron looked at his dad and thought to himself how old his dad looked. It seemed like he had aged so much in the last few years. Cameron and Tyler owed so much to their father. Spending the last few years with the man they loved more than anything in the world was the least they could do.

Cameron and Tyler kept a constant watch on Shane and Sylvia. It wasn't too long after they moved that they noticed Shane and Sylvia were at the age when they shouldn't be living by themselves. They were getting forgetful and several times, they noticed that Sylvia had left one of the stove burners on. It was something that Cameron and Tyler were becoming more fearful of. They needed to do something. There comes a time in people's lives when they have to realize they can't do things on their own anymore. Shane and Sylvia needed to be cared for. The hardest time in Cameron's and Tyler's lives was when they told Shane and Sylvia that they couldn't live alone in their condominium any longer.

Chapter Forty-Nine

Cameron and Tyler loved their dad and Sylvia. They wanted to do what they could to help them. They looked at nursing homes and assisted living communities in the area. They both decided that they could get around fairly well – even at their ages. To them, a nursing home seemed too restrictive. They narrowed it down to three assisted living communities in the area. The first thing they needed to do was talk with their dad. Shane knew that what they were doing was in the best interest of everyone concerned.

Shane and Sylvia agreed that they would look at the three communities that the boys thought would be best for them. Two of them seemed to have the nursing home atmosphere but were too restrictive. The last community that they looked at was one they loved. There were many activities planned for the seniors. *Seniors, that's really us. We are very senior,* thought Shane. The boys knew that Shane and Sylvia had to move, but they wanted to give them some time to talk it over between themselves. The couple eventually called Cameron and Tyler and told them that they decided on the last assisted living community. They liked the fact that many activities were planned, they could still leave and use their own car, Sylvia wouldn't have to make meals anymore, and nursing care was available around the clock.

Tyler was looking at a late night movie in which the main character was a rich man in the same situation as his dad. His family talked about putting him in an assisted living community as well. One of his sons and his daughter had talked and it was decided that instead of moving their father, why couldn't they get a live-in caregiver for their father?

Tyler said, "That's it! Why do we need to move Dad and Sylvia?" Tyler couldn't wait any longer. He called Cameron very late at night. Tyler said, "Cameron, we're making a terrible mistake." Tyler explained to Cameron what he had seen on the movie.

"Dad is a very wealthy man," said Cameron. "You are right, Tyler. They don't need to move. A caregiver can clean the apartment, cook the meals, and keep a check on dad and Sylvia's medication. Besides, a caregiver would keep both of them company." Both of the boys thought it was a wonderful idea. They decided that in the morning, they would go by the condo and see what their dad and Sylvia thought of the idea.

The boys arrived around mid-morning and said they needed to talk to both of them. Cameron said, "Tyler came up with a great idea last night so you won't have to move out of the condo. Let us know what you think of it?" Tyler told them of what he had seen on the movie. Both boys told their dad that he was a very wealthy man and could surely afford a live-in caregiver.

Sylvia smiled at Shane and added, "I think it is a great idea, don't you Shane?" Shane agreed right away, letting the boys know that they really didn't want to move anyway.

"Let us take care of trying to find someone and the final decision on who to hire will be up to the two of you," Tyler said. It was the same day that the search was started by Cameron and Tyler.

They located a woman who was middle-aged and had done the job of being a caregiver several times before. Cameron and Tyler thought she would be the perfect one. It was arranged for her to meet them at the condo late one afternoon. Tyler said, "Dad and Sylvia, this is Jessica Pearson. She would like to work for you. Jessica has experience in doing the job and has no problem with doing the other needed duties around here."

"Nice to meet you, Mr. and Mrs. Donaldson," Jessica said.

"We aren't formal around here," said Shane. "The first thing you have to do is call us by our first names." There were three bedrooms in the Donaldsons' apartment. Shane told her one of the spare bedrooms was a guest room in case one of the boys wanted to come and visit. He then said, "We have a few things stored in the third bedroom." Shane agreed that the boys could help clean it out and set up a room for Jessica.

Jessica told all of them that she was widowed. Her husband had a serious illness and didn't recover from the operation. "He died about two years ago," she said. She told them that she was lonesome living alone and would love to have the job if they approved of her qualifications.

"Jessica, could you excuse us for a few minutes while the rest of us talk together?" Cameron said. She excused herself and went out into the hallway. It was only a few minutes before Shane asked her to please come back in.

"I'm sorry about asking you to go in the hallway for a few minutes," Shane said. Jessica told him that she didn't mind. "Jessica, we were considering on moving to an assisted living community. That was an option, but we would much rather stay here. I guess Cameron and Tyler had explained what would be expected of you here. We would like this to be your home, as well as ours. We do expect that things get done and that we are looked after in our old age. Jessica, if you would like the job, it's yours," said Shane. Jessica accepted immediately. Within just a few days, new furniture arrived and the spare room was set up for Jessica.

Jessica arrived the following day and was ready to start work. She immediately felt like she had made the right decision. Shane and Sylvia liked having her around. She was doing a great job of keeping the place clean and she prepared great meals. The food shopping was her job. It made Sylvia happy, because she didn't have to deal with it any longer. Cameron called a few days after Jessica started and wanted to know how she was working out. Shane said, "She is wonderful, Cameron. She is a hard worker, keeps the place spotless, and what a wonderful cook she is! I'm glad that Tyler came up with the idea."

"So am I, Dad," Cameron replied. "I thought it was a wonderful idea as soon as he mentioned it to me." Having Jessica living with Shane and Sylvia gave Cameron, Tyler, Heather, and Beth much more peace of mind.

Weeks turned into months and before they knew it, Jessica had been working there a year. Shane called her into the living room one day. Sylvia sat down beside him. They both told Jessica how pleased they were. She said, "I was scared. I thought you were going to fire me."

They all laughed as Shane said to her, "Not at all. In fact, we are very pleased with your work." He handed her an envelope and told her it was just a little bonus for doing such a good job. Jessica thanked them and retreated to her room.

She sat down on the edge of her bed and opened the envelope. She was surprised to see that they had given her a check for a thousand dollars as a bonus. She immediately went back out to the living room and told them, "Thank you so much! I really appreciate it." They were pleased to do it. After all, good work should be rewarded – Shane always thought.

It was harder for Shane and Sylvia to walk around anymore. Cameron and Tyler decided to get each of them a power wheelchair for Christmas. They told them that they didn't have to use them all the time, just when they felt tired or they didn't want to walk a long distance. They were glad to get them and people would see them racing through the halls. Shane and Sylvia thought they were the greatest. As they were racing about, they would laugh and laugh. The boys could see that they hadn't been that happy in years.

Chapter Fifty

Shane and Sylvia were closing in on ninety. They weren't there yet, but it would only be a little over a year when Shane hit the magic number. Shane and Sylvia both had minds as sharp as a tack. They could hold a conversation that sometimes seemed hard for Cameron and Tyler to keep up with. Shane and Sylvia played bingo in the downstairs community room every Friday night. It helped to keep them so sharp and nothing made Sylvia happier than winning a two hundred dollar jackpot. It was fun for them. Shane always had this saying that "age means nothing." He would say, "Growing old is just another chapter in your life. As long as it isn't the final chapter, then you are doing fine." He did at times wonder how long it would be until that final chapter came.

Jessica enjoyed both of them so much. They treated her more like a daughter than an employee. That seemed to be what Jessica liked the most. It didn't seem like a job to her. She felt more like part of the family. That was the working atmosphere that Shane wanted to give Jessica. It was the same feeling Shane got when he worked for Paul at the Scenic View Inn. Paul treated him so well. It was more like they were brothers. Shane had been very fortunate in his working life. Few people could say that they enjoyed every boss they had. Paul and Shane often sat in the rocking chairs on the front porch of the inn and chatted, laughed, and just had a good time. Shane would never forget how well Paul had treated him.

Around the middle of the summer, Shane didn't feel well sometimes. He went to the doctor and had some tests run, but nothing showed any problems. He thought, *maybe this is how I should feel as I'm approaching ninety.* He got around well, especially with his power chair. His feelings changed like the weather. One day, he felt great and other days, he just had that ill feeling all over – like he didn't feel well. Sylvia attended to him like she wanted to. She knew it was Jessica's job, but there were certain things that she still wanted to do herself. Jessica just smiled and didn't say a word. She knew how much Sylvia loved Shane.

One night, while Shane and Sylvia were watching a movie on television, Shane got up and said he wasn't feeling very well and decided to go to bed early. He gave Sylvia a kiss on the cheek and said, "I'll see you in bed, honey."

She smiled and said, "I'm going to see the end of this movie and then I'll be right in." When she went to bed about a half an hour later she could see that Shane was fast asleep. She got into bed quietly, so she didn't wake him up. After only a few minutes, she dozed off too.

Sylvia woke up just as the sun was coming up. She hit Shane on the back and said, "Let's get up, sleepyhead." He didn't move. She felt him and rolled him over on his back. She had tears streaming down her cheeks. Shane was dead. He had died in his sleep sometime during the night. Sylvia started to scream, "Jessica, Jessica, come here! I need you Jessica!" Jessica came running into the room. Sylvia said, "He's dead, Jessica. What am I going to do?"

Jessica took Sylvia out into the living room and called 9-1-1. Jessica then called Cameron, and Tyler. Tyler was the first one to arrive. He did what he could to console Sylvia. She was hysterical, but Tyler did what he could. The police and an ambulance arrived and Tyler told them that Shane had died in his sleep. Cameron came in and went to Tyler and Sylvia. He said, "I'm so sorry, Sylvia. Don't you worry. We'll take care of all the arrangements." She was thanking them, just as Heather and Beth came into the apartment.

Cameron and Tyler got up and went to the police and paramedics as Heather and Beth sat down with Sylvia. She kept asking what she was going to do without Shane. Jessica got done talking with the police. Then she went to sit down with Sylvia, too. Cameron and Tyler couldn't believe their dad was gone. Both of them always felt like he would live forever. He seemed larger than life to them – every day. The paramedics arranged to have the body removed. It wasn't long before Cameron and Tyler were at the funeral home making the arrangements. It was Shane's wish to be cremated and have his ashes sprinkled behind a rock in Vermont where he had sprinkled Gina's ashes.

Sylvia was visibly shaken. First Peggy, then Paul, and now Shane had all died. She was the only one left of the fearless four. When she thought of them, it made her smile. The funeral was lovely. So many friends attended. Sylvia sat there and was grateful that they had made so many friends in Florida, considering that they had only lived there a short time. Shane was cremated. Cameron talked with Sylvia. She already knew of Shane's wishes. He had told her a long time ago. Cameron and Tyler spent some time with Sylvia before they made the trip to Vermont. They arrived at their cabin in Vermont late in the evening.

The next morning, Tyler carried the urn and Shane Donaldson's two sons made the long walk to the trail. They had to walk it. It was a "walk to love," as Shane always told them. They came to the rock and Cameron and Tyler made a pile of leaves. It was a huge pile – just the way Shane had told Cameron how he wanted it to be. Cameron took the urn and spread half of the ashes on the pile. He then handed the urn to Tyler who spread the rest of the ashes about. He then laid the empty urn next to Gina's, which had been sitting there for many years now. No one had bothered it and now, Shane and Gina were together forever. It was a fitting end to a love between two people that stretched many years.

Cameron and Tyler sat down against a couple of trees with tears running down their cheeks. They just sat there and stared at the pile of leaves for the longest time. All of a sudden, Cameron got a little smile on his face and then proceeded to laugh so loud. Tyler looked at him and said, "What's so funny? This is a sad day."

"Tyler, look at that pile of leaves. If you made a pile of leaves like that and had a girl here, what would you be doing?" Cameron said.

"Oh my God! They did it right here!" Tyler said. "That's what was so special to Dad about this spot. They did it right here!" Cameron and Tyler were both laughing. They sat there for the longest time, just smiling and knowing that their mom and dad had a good time on a pile of leaves behind that rock.

Cameron and Tyler left the next morning to go back to Florida. The first thing they did was to check in on Sylvia. They loved her just like she was their real mother. Shane's attorney took care of Shane's estate. He did have a considerable amount of money and the apartment in the condo in Florida. That was pretty much the extent of his holdings. His will gave Cameron and Tyler each a half a million dollars. The rest would provide for Sylvia to remain in her residence until her death. When Sylvia's death should occur, the funeral and burial would be taken care of. After Sylvia's death, any money left over would go to the Gina Donaldson Foundation for the Terminally Ill. Shane had talked profusely with his attorney and Sylvia about how he wished his will to be carried out. Sylvia was pleased and went along with Shane's wishes.

Sylvia kept Jessica on as her caregiver. Jessica was happy and spent as much time with Sylvia as she could. Sylvia was never the same after Shane's death. Often, she thought back to the first time she laid eyes on him at the roadside stand in Alabama. She would smile and say, "He was a handsome man; a very handsome man."

Chapter Fifty-One

Shane had finally come to that final chapter in his life that he often talked about. If one was to look back on Shane's life, he would say it was amazing. Happiness, sorrow, writing a book, helping to start a foundation in his wife's honor were all part of his life. He wasn't a flashy man and never liked the spotlight that fell on him after he wrote his book. It was his legacy – to spend many years giving speeches and privately talking with families that had terminally ill family members. Hundreds of families were helped by his private talks. He knew it was a terrible thing not to know where to turn. God had a purpose in his life and it was his destiny to fulfill that purpose.

Cameron and Tyler continued to carry on the Donaldson name. Cameron had a son who would never let the Donaldson legacy fade away. He would always remember his grandpa who told him stories of when he was a little boy. Heather and Beth were wonderful daughters-in-law to Shane. They showed him so much caring as he advanced in his senior years. Florida would remain Cameron and Tyler and their wives' home for the rest of their lives. They liked it there, knowing it was where their daddy had walked his last steps and taken his final breath. It brought tears to their eyes sometimes, especially when they looked at family photos. It gave Cameron and Tyler memories of their youth in Change, Kansas and then later growing up in the mountains of Vermont. They always thought of the way their mom and dad had taught them the values of life. It instilled in them a sense of pride in anything they would ever do.

Sylvia remained living in the condo apartment for a few years. Jessica was always by her side, knowing that she would someday see the last line written in Sylvia's final chapter. Before that day came, they enjoyed each other's company. Jessica loved listening to Sylvia tell stories: the sad story of how her husband was killed in the war; the interesting story of how she met Shane and then he walked out of her life; and also, the story of when she read his book and then made the trip to Vermont to visit him over twenty-five years after their first meeting.

Shane Donaldson was just an ordinary man who was depressed after his first wife was killed in a car accident. It was a time when life didn't seem worth living. God came to him and sent him on a journey that extended half way across America. It was a walking journey that gave him a better sense of feeling about himself and taught him respect for other people. So many people in Change, Kansas gave him happiness every day. It was in Change that he met the woman of his life. He loved his other two wives very much. However, it was a young woman named Gina Albertson who walked into his life like no other person ever had. She had much heartbreak in her young life. Shane changed her life around just as much as she changed his.

He loved Vermont and met Paul and Peggy who ran the Scenic View Inn. He loved the beautiful mountains and spent many hours there working and walking the trails. Sylvia had come to him there and eased the heartbreak following Gina's death. Sylvia was his third wife. Shane was a rugged, muscular man in his younger years. He had been married three times – to women who made him smile, who made him want to get up each day, and who made him treat them with the love and kindness that they deserved.

There wasn't a bad bone in Shane Donaldson's body. He lived every day to the fullest.

Sylvia became very ill three years after Shane's death. She couldn't walk and was in the final stages of Alzheimer's disease. It was tough on Jessica to see not only her employer, but her best friend, go downhill so fast. Jessica knew it was just a matter of time before Sylvia needed better care than she could provide. Jessica had a talk with Cameron and Tyler and told them that Sylvia really should be in a nursing home. They told her that they would see about getting Sylvia in a nursing home that would provide that care. Sylvia looked so frail to them. She didn't really know them anymore. It was sad to see in a woman who was so vibrant when they first met her. Cameron and Tyler had much stress put on them the last few years because of the death of their dad. Now, Sylvia needed help and it was up to the boys to see that she got it. As the boys thought back – and Jessica, too, they realized they didn't pick up on the early stages of the disease.

Sylvia was placed in a nursing home. She had a living will made out that specified she was not to be kept alive by artificial means. Sylvia remained in that nursing home for almost three years. She was visited by Cameron, Tyler, one of their wives, or Jessica every day until her death on a rainy Florida night. Her desire was to be buried back in her hometown in Alabama. The boys made those arrangements and attended her funeral and burial in her hometown. They knew it would have meant a lot to her. She had been so good to the boys and treated them so well. She treated them as though they were her own, and the boys would always be thankful for that.

It was the final chapter in the lives of Shane and Sylvia Donaldson. Shane and Sylvia grew old together. They were happy and loved each other. What more could anyone ask for in the latter stages of their lives? It had been amazing for them to spend many years in the mountains of Vermont. Their final years in Florida were saddened with the death of Peggy, followed by Paul's suicide. It seemed like after the deaths of their best friends, they no longer had the great outlook on life that they shared for many years.

The vicious cycle will never end. People have been born and died since the beginning of human life on this planet we call earth. Cameron and Tyler knew that Shane, Becky, Gina, Sylvia, Peggy, and Paul would all be together again in heaven. At night, the boys would often look up at the stars, smile and say, "We love you all. We'll never forget you." The story in the life of one amazing man has finished the final chapter.

It has been estimated that since the beginning of human life there have been approximately 105 billion people that have lived on earth. Just imagine if everyone only had one story to tell. The stories would boggle the mind. This was just a story of one man's life. Do you have a story to tell? Would you walk halfway across America? Would you walk to love? He did and he never regretted it for one second. Shane always had God in his life – teaching him, guiding him, and loving him. God knew it was time to let Shane enter His place.

CPSIA information can be obtained
at www.ICGtesting.com
Printed in the USA
BVOW08s1926221116

468642BV00001B/19/P